THE DOCTOR'S NANNY

A SINGLE DAD & NANNY ROMANCE (SAVED BY THE DOCTOR 3)

MICHELLE LOVE
IVY WONDER

CONTENTS

Blurb	v
1. Alex	1
2. Ky	7
3. Alex	13
4. Ky	19
5. Alex	26
6. Ky	31
7. Alex	37
8. Ky	43
9. Alex	49
10. Ky	54
11. Alex	60
12. Ky	66
13. Alex	72
14. Ky	78
15. Alex	84
16. Ky	89
17. Alex	95
18. Ky	101
19. Alex	106
20. Ky	112
21. Alex	118
22. Ky	123
23. Alex	128
24. Ky	134
25. Alex	140
26. Ky	145
27. Alex	151
28. Ky	157
29. Alex	163
30. Ky	168
Sneak Peek - Jade	172

Made in "The United States" by:

Michelle Love & Ivy Wonder

© Copyright 2020

ISBN: 9781648081316

ALL RIGHTS RESERVED. No part of this publication may be reproduced or transmitted in any form whatsoever, electronic, or mechanical, including photocopying, recording, or by any informational storage or retrieval system without express written, dated and signed permission from the author

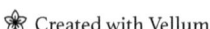 Created with Vellum

BLURB

Premise

When the father of a three-year-old daughter loses his wife to cancer, he takes a year off work to grieve. As a neurosurgeon, he's ready to get back to work and accepts a job at Saint Christopher's General Hospital in Seattle, Washington.

After hiring a nanny who's fresh out of college, he finds her innocence bewitching. She's a virgin who's never had an orgasm and the two share the attraction. But nannies are not supposed to get involved with their bosses.

When the doctor is hit by a car one day, she fears she might lose him. When his old in-laws come to take his daughter away, thinking it's the best thing for the little girl, the nanny is left alone in the big house she's begun to think of as home for her and the man and child she loves.

Will he survive, and if so, can their love go on? Or will she lose him and the child she's come to think of as her own, for good?

She was there for me, but she wasn't supposed to make me feel the way she did...
When my wife died, it left a hole the size of Texas in my heart.
Alone with our young daughter, I needed assistance.
That's when I found her.
Or did she find me? Young, beautiful, and insightful beyond her years, she saved me from making a terrible mistake.
Did I make one anyway when I hired her and brought her into my home?
It didn't feel like a mistake when I took her into my arms and showed her what it's like to be a woman.
In my lifetime I'd learned when things are going great, something happens to make it disappear.
Would it happen to me again?

Lusting after the boss wasn't what I was supposed to do...
Hired to care for his young daughter, I shouldn't have looked at him the way I did.
Everything about the man fascinated me.
When he touched me, unimaginable things happened to my young and innocent body.
He taught me things I'd never knew existed.
He took my heart and made it his, the same as he did with my willing body.
But he seemed to be cursed where love was concerned.
And I had to wonder if that curse would slip over me.
Would our love last...or would it end with tragedy and loss?

1
ALEX

A SOFT RAIN fell as I made my way into Saint Christopher's General Hospital in Seattle, Washington. I was there to meet with the board about getting rights to practice in the hospital, but I wasn't looking forward to pleading my case to anyone.

She died a year ago and I was ready to move on with my life again. Yet there was some opposition to me getting back to work. Not many men bury their wives when they're only twenty-nine-years-old.

Rachelle had all the money in the world, but none of it could save her from ovarian cancer. She left me and our daughter, three-years-old now, and the empty space she left felt enormous. I was tired of looking at all the places she'd left empty—her side of our bed being at the top of that list.

A woman's smile greeted me from behind the information desk. "Good morning, sir. How can I help you today?"

"I have a meeting with Doctors Kerr and Dawson." I ran my hand through my hair, then shoved them both into my pockets.

"Which Dr. Dawson?" she asked. "We have two of them."

"His first name is Harris. Who's the other one?"

"His wife, Dr. Reagan Storey-Dawson is a cardiologist here." She looked through the notepad on the desk, then pointed at the hallway to the right. "Down that hall, the second door on the right." She took a sip of coffee. "Dr. Alexander Arlen. That's you, right? You have a meeting about getting privileges. I look forward to seeing you around."

As I straightened my tie, she checked for a wedding ring, of which I had none. "I haven't got the job yet, Miss."

"Miss Sandoval. Lydia Sandoval," she said. "Single."

"Okay." I turned to leave, feeling a little awkward about the exchange.

"And you?" she called out cheerfully after me.

"Same." I didn't want to get into my personal situation any further, afraid she might ask me out, and I wasn't ready to go out with anyone. Not yet—maybe not ever.

I loved my wife. The last two years of her life were spent in and out of the hospital and doctors' offices. Those years were miserable on her and me equally. There was nothing left in me to give to anyone else. Maybe time would help. All I knew was I needed to get back to work—my work – or I'd go crazy.

As I walked into the small conference room, the two men scheduled to grill me were already there. Both tall and lean, they were standing as I walked in. One of them extended his hand. "Dr. Harris Dawson, Dr. Arlen."

"Nice to meet you, Dr. Dawson," I greeted him then held out my hand to the other man. "And you must be Dr. Jonas Kerr."

"I am." He shook my hand. "It's a pleasure to meet you, Dr. Arlen."

Dr. Dawson took a seat. "Let's put all this formality aside, shall we? I'm Harris and this is Jonas. Is that okay with you, Alexander?"

"Call me Alex." I took a seat on the opposite side of the table from the two men. "And dropping formalities is great with me."

Jonas wore a smile as he asked, "How was the trip into town, Alex?"

I had flown our private jet from Spokane—where we lived—to Seattle. I wanted to get out of that city. Reminders of my wife were everywhere. It proved to be maddening. "It was fine. I made it in record time. The wind was with us."

Harris nodded, "And if you're approved to practice here, would you relocate to Seattle?"

"I would." I should be honest with the men. "Look, you might know about my wife's passing. Living in Spokane just isn't the same. Everywhere I look, Rachelle is there in some form or another. I need to get out of there."

The two exchanged looks. Then Harris asked, "How about your daughter, Alex? You'd be taking her away from family, wouldn't you?"

"My wife's parents live in Spokane, about a mile away from us." They probably don't want me to leave with Tabby, but I had to do what was best for myself. I'd given up a lot during the last few years, and it was time to get back on track. My daughter would be fine with me and my choices. We shared a mutual adoration that told me she'd be great as long as she was with me.

Looking concerned, Jonas asked, "Moving may adversely affect your young daughter, Alex. Having her mother's parents in her life is important. Do you suppose taking her away is the right thing to do?"

"My daughter—her name's Tabitha—she and I have a special bond. I've cared for her all alone since Rachelle got sick immediately after her birth. She's not as close to her grandparents." Rachelle's parents weren't always around. They traveled extensively, and when not doing that, they were involved in all kinds of events. Being from old money, they had their hands in all sorts of charitable organizations. It kept them pretty busy.

Harris got right to the point, "You must've inherited your wife's fortune, Alex. From what I've read about the Vanderhavens, their net worth is in the billions. Your wife was their only child. I'm sure her portion of that wasn't chump change."

He was right. When Rachelle passed on, I'd become a very rich man. "While more than comfortable financially, I'm not the kind of man who stops working because he has enough money to do so. My brain needs more than that." Being a neurosurgeon himself, Harris should empathize.

His nod told me he understood. "I have a more than comfortable financial status that has nothing to do with my work as a doctor, so I understand where you're coming from. But I wasn't responsible for a young child on my own either. So my next question is, what will you do with young Tabitha when you're working?"

I'd thought about that a lot—more anything else. "I'll hire a live-in nanny to help me with Tabby."

Jonas nodded as he smiled. "That's good. I'd hate to think of your daughter having to go to daycare after losing her mother. She needs a stable female presence in her life. If not her grandmother, then a nanny—the right one of course—would be best."

I thought so too. "That's another reason to get away from Spokane. My in-laws aren't around much. Tabby needs a woman's influence in her life. A nanny would help immensely."

Harris still seemed skeptical. "What about *your* family, Alex? Is anyone available from your side to be that female presence for your daughter?"

I shook my head. "No sisters, only one younger brother. And Mom and Dad have their own things to do. They live in Colorado. The three of them moved there after the legalization of marijuana. They have a dispensary there now."

Jonas grinned. "One of *those* kinds of stores?"

"Yep." My family got into the marijuana trade, and business is very good. "While I'm happy my family has found their calling, it's not the right kind of world for my kid to grow up in. Not that I'm judging. I just want a different life for my child and me."

Harris agreed, "Yeah, I can see that. So, you've been thinking about this for a while. You're not making any rash decisions or running away, you just want to change your life a bit, to get away from all the reminders of a lost love."

"Yes." I was tired of living in the place I once shared with the woman I'd fallen in love with, practically at first sight. "It's time to start fresh. And I'd love to make that fresh start right here with you guys in this hospital where I can help the most people while still having time for my daughter."

"How much time would you need to relocate and get settled here, Alex?" Harris asked.

Good question. He's considering me. "A month." It would take that amount of time to find a suitable home and a babysitter, too. I wouldn't leave Tabby with anyone but the one I hired. I want her to feel stable and safe. Having her doted on by too many people would undermine her security. I didn't want that.

Harris tapped his pencil on the pad of paper in front of him. "We'll give you two months to be on the safe side." He looked at me. "I'm a father, too. You'll need time to make sure your daughter is settled well with the new living situation and her nanny. So, we'll see you here in two months. And if you want my advice on finding adequate housing, check out Janelle's Real Estate Agency. She's a natural when it comes to finding homes for Seattle's more affluent residents."

Jonas gave me another big smile. "Welcome aboard, Dr. Alex Arlen."

"I can't thank you two enough." I got up, shook both their hands and felt a smile plaster across my face. "This is such good news. You have no idea how excited I am to be coming here."

Jonas stood. "The rain isn't going to bother you?"

"I love it." I never minded rain. The smell of it invigorated me in a way little else did. "I can't wait to get things in order and get my life going again. It's been an eternity since I got to be me."

"Well, it's not just you, Alex," Harris reminded me. "Keep your daughter at the top of your list."

"I am." He had no idea how much *at the top* Tabby was. "Tabby's my only link left to Rachelle. She's the spitting image of her mother. It's funny, when I see things around our home and the town she had so much to do with, I feel sad. But when I look at our daughter and see her mother in her, it makes me happy."

Jonas looked at me with sad eyes. "I can't imagine what it must feel like to lose someone at such a young age. No one expects to be thirty-something and a widower with a small child."

"No, you don't." If anyone would've told me Rachelle and I would only have two years of marriage before she was stricken with a cancer so fierce nothing could combat it, I would've said they were crazy.

Harris patted me on the back. "Life will be different here. No ghosts to torment you, Alex."

No ghosts?

Did I truly want to leave Rachelle behind?

Our bed proved to be a place I hardly ever rested anymore because I felt her in it. I would wake up, think I could hear her breathing, then reach out to find no one there.

In a new place, a new bed, I wouldn't feel her there. *Is that what I really want?*

Am I ready to do this? Or is this a terrible mistake?

2
KY

"The bathroom's free," my roommate, Carla, called out to me.

"Thanks, Carla." Grabbing my clothes for the day, I took my turn in the bathroom.

Four of us shared the two bedroom, one bath apartment I leased after my graduation. I got my bachelor's degree in early childhood development, and now I just waited for my first opportunity.

I signed up with an employment agency that specialized in finding jobs for *au pairs*. And I already landed my first interview. A new doctor had moved to Seattle and needed a live-in governess for his three-year-old daughter.

As I showered, I tried not to get my hopes up too high; that job must be coveted by many. To reside in the posh house of a doctor would be like a dream come true.

I'd grown up in a modest home in Seattle's Ballard neighborhood. My father worked as a parts manager at a car dealership. Mom worked at a health food store as a cashier. I worked my way through college with a job at the same store as Mom. Living at home allowed me to pay my way through school and avoid getting into debt to get my degree. I had Mom and Dad to thank for that.

Well, them, and some sacrifices of my own. I sold my car and bought a bus pass instead. Making payments on the car and insurance didn't leave me much, so getting rid of it allowed me to spend more on my coursework. Plus, I always took my own sack lunch and never went out, choosing to use my funds on opportunities.

After college, I continued working at the store for another year. With no debt, I was able to move in with my friends at their steady coaxing. Carla was my bestie, and she said I wasn't being true to myself by living at home. She claimed it stunted my natural human growth.

My lack of experience with any type of physical intimacy seemed to concern her. Carla was a psych major, and emotional health was of utmost value to her. She claimed I wasn't emotionally healthy.

I pushed back that one does not need sex to be emotionally fit. She didn't believe that whatsoever; Carla considered sex a mandatory experience. And she made sure to experience it with all sorts of people, females included. I wasn't into that type of experience.

In my opinion, my virginity didn't define me. Apparently, to some, virginity was a thing you got rid of as soon as you got the chance. Not me. I wasn't about to have sex with someone I didn't have feelings for. It was too personal to do with just anyone.

A knock on the bathroom door had me speeding up. "I'm almost done."

"Okay, try to hurry, please!" my other roomy, Lane, said. "I've got to pee."

Having only one bathroom sucked. Without putting the conditioner in my hair, I got out and dried off, hurrying to get dressed and out of the way.

Looking at my reflection, I wasn't going to look my best for the interview, but being so rushed, I had no choice. Leaving the bathroom, I went to my bedroom to put my hair into a bun and a touch of mascara on my lashes before leaving the apartment.

A cool, misty rain fell from the sky that morning. It was invigorating and made me feel better about the day. Everyone looks dewy in this type of weather, not just me.

As I walked to the bus stop, I tried not to think about the interview. I worried that this father might pick someone older and more experienced.

At twenty-two, with no practice, my chances were slim to none. But the lady at the employment agency said that even the experience of interviewing was beneficial to me. It may help me to do better on future interviews.

Getting off the bus at the employment agency, I started to feel a little sick to my stomach. My nerves surprised me. I never had an interview before! Not even for the job at the store. Mom arranged that for me. I had nothing to do but show up.

A shiny black Jaguar sedan was parked in front. I instinctively knew it belonged to the man who needed a nanny. He had to be even wealthier than I imagined. And now the butterflies in my stomach swarmed me so much I ran to the agency's bathroom first.

My cheeks were flushed, so I splashed some cold water on my face. Looking in the mirror, I gave myself a pep talk. "Look, Ky, this is just practice. You're not getting this job, so be cool. Get this over with and don't freak out. You don't have the experience to get this work. This is like we practiced back in school. It's all pretend."

With that idea in my head, I dried my face then went out to let the receptionist know I arrived. She'd seen me dash into the bathroom and looked disapprovingly. "And your name is?"

"Kyla Rush." I didn't know what to do with my hands all of a sudden and stuffed them into the pockets of my blue jeans. "I'm here for an interview with Dr. Arlen for the position of governess."

Her eyes scanned my body. "Wearing jeans and a sweater?"

Scanning my clothing choice, I hadn't found it to be bad. "The jeans aren't ripped or dirty. And the sweater covers my chest. What's wrong with it?"

The woman, who looked to be in her forties, only shook her head. "Kids."

And there it was. I knew I'd never get the job. Not when I looked like a kid. Who would trust a kid to take care of their kid?

Certainly not some rich doctor.

"I'll take a seat," I told her, then walked away, not interested in being judged by her any longer.

I mean who does she think she is anyway? Forty-something and just a receptionist at an employment agency where she has opportunities to take better jobs?

I couldn't let her get to me. And this was only a practice run for me anyway. So what if she didn't think I was dressed appropriately!

The outside door opened and a woman walked in, wearing a dark blue dress that went below her knees. Her shoes were flat, blue, and sensible. The creases around her mouth looked like parentheses. She was all of fifty and looked it. "I'm here to see Dr. Arlen for the *au pair* position."

The receptionist smiled, looking pleased with this new candidate. "Oh, yes. You must be Mrs. Steiner. Your experience is outstanding."

"Yes, it is," the woman agreed. She looked around the room, empty but for me. I received only the slightest glance, before she looked back at the receptionist. "Are we the only people being interviewed for this position?"

"There's one more," the receptionist informed her. "A man."

Looking down her nose, the professional nanny seemed unimpressed. "A man? I see." She went to take a seat on the other side of the room.

While I played a game on my cell phone, she looked out the window at the rain that had become a bit more than the light mist it had been earlier. Then her gaze fell on me, and I looked at her. "Hi."

She nodded. "Hello."

When the door opened again, and a tall, thin man came in, she sighed, and I gathered she'd seen the guy before. He looked directly at her and sighed, too. "So, you've got an interview, too, Sally?"

With a nod, she said, "Yes. I had no idea you were free from your duties to apply for this position. What happened with the Ventura children?"

"Sheila quit her job to stay home with them when Emily started wetting the bed." He went to the receptionist, his hands running over the front of the suit he wore. "Manly Jones to interview with Dr. Arlen."

"Yes, sir," she told him. "Take a seat. Since you're all here, I'll let him know, and we can start the interviews."

He walked over to sit near the other woman, and I saw he was nearer to her age than mine. "And what has you free, Sally?"

"Elias went into high school this year and no longer needs a sitter."

Nodding, he understood. Those two had oodles of experience, while I had none. And when the man's eyes landed on me, I felt unspeakably inept. "Have you ever done this before?" he asked.

I shook my head. "First interview."

Sally decided to ask me a question, "And what makes you think you're capable of being a governess?"

"I have a bachelor's in early childhood development," I whispered insecurely.

"Education?" the man asked. "That makes you a viable candidate?"

Shrugging, I didn't know what to say. I wasn't a viable candidate. Especially now that I was up against them. Both had lots of experience and the doctor would be foolish not to hire one of them. My bets were on Sally just because she was a woman.

But then again, what would the mother of this child want? And I had no idea why she wasn't mentioned as an interviewer. Surely the mother of this child wanted to be involved in picking a suitable nanny for her little girl.

They might want a man to watch over their child. Maybe they would feel she'd be more protected that way? The guy looks kind of buff. He gave off an air of protection, too.

A door to the back opened and another woman stood there. "Mrs. Sally Steiner?"

Sally got up and followed her, leaving Manly Jones and me alone. "How old are you?" he asked me.

"Twenty-two." An interview with a competitor before the actual interview. Terrific. "And you?"

"Forty-three," he said. "I've been doing this type of work since I was ten raising my younger brothers when our mother overdosed on opiates. We avoided getting sent to a children's home for nearly a year, because I kept things going so well. Nobody knew no one took care of us."

I found that hard to believe. "Is that the story you tell?"

His dark eyes leveled on mine. "Young lady, that is no story. That is the God's honest truth."

"How'd a ten-year-old pay bills?" I asked cocking one brow at him. I knew a liar when I heard one.

He turned to look out the window. "You would never understand what it was like when I was a kid. Bills? How can one have bills when one has no home?"

"So, you took care of your younger siblings as you lived on the street?" I still didn't believe him. "And at ten-years'-old?"

All he did was nod as he wouldn't look at me anymore. And that bothered me none at all. What did bother me was thinking that this man might get the job. And him taking care of a little girl didn't sit right with me.

3

ALEX

I ALREADY HAD three days of interviews for the *au pair* position and had yet to find the perfect one for Tabby. This fourth one has to be the last. With only a couple of weeks left until I start work, I wanted someone right away. That way Tabby would have time with me around, to get used to another person taking care of her.

A fifty-year-old woman walked into the small interview room. Her graying hair in a neat bun, she wore what I'd call typical governess clothing and a stoic expression to match. "Dr. Arlen, I'm Mrs. Steiner." She extended her hand as I rose.

Shaking it, I noticed the lack of a smile on her face. "It's nice to meet you, Mrs. Steiner." Her resume was impeccable. She'd been the governess for many important families in the Seattle area. But I still wasn't sure about her. "Please take a seat."

She sat across from me, her hands placed neatly in her lap. "I see you have my resume there in front of you. I'd like to point out my years of experience. The last four pages are letters of recommendation from my past employers. All of the children I had the pleasure of helping raise have gone to college. Well, except Elias, but he's still in high school. He'll go as well. My purpose is to compel education upon my charges."

I had no idea what charges were. "Your charges?"

She looked at me with dark brown eyes, surrounded by thin lines. "The children I look after, sir."

"Okay." That told me she wasn't close to the kids she helped raise. "And you like to make sure they seek further education?" That wasn't such a bad thing.

"I have." She pointed at the resume in front of me again. "If you'll read the first recommendation, I started working with those children when the oldest was only four. The three of them were well versed in the Bible as well as proper behavior."

"And how about playing?" That was more important to me than behaving. Tabby wasn't a bad child in the first place.

"A time and a place for that are scheduled into each day." She looked me in the eyes. "I've been a nanny for longer than you've been a father. I can help take this great burden off your shoulders, Doctor. That way you can do your work. And your wife can as well."

"I don't have one." And Tabby is not a burden. "I tell you what, Mrs. Steiner, I've got your resume and will study it before making my decision. Thank you for coming."

She seemed a bit shocked as she sat there. "So, this is it?"

I nodded and got up to walk her out. "It is."

"I never had such a short interview before, sir." She got up, and I escorted her to the door. "Is there anything else I can answer for you?"

I had one more question, not that it would matter, but I wanted to know. "And how are you on corporal punishment?"

"Spare the rod, spoil the child," she said quickly.

Thought so.

"You have a wonderful day, Mrs. Steiner." I closed the door behind her, not missing the stunned expression she wore.

Going back to the table, I tossed her resume aside. No one would be laying a hand on my baby girl.

There was a quick knock at the door and then a tall man opened it and stepped in. I had Manly Jones' resume pulled out of the file. The receptionist had sorted them in the order they would be interviewed. "Mr. Jones, it's nice to meet you." I got up and shook his hand.

"You, too, Doc," he said with a smoothness that made him seem down to Earth.

"Please, take a seat." I took mine, then looked over his resume. "Seems you've watched over quite a few kids in your time, Manly." *How did he get into the babysitting business?* "And you came to be an *au pair* how exactly?"

"As you can see on my resume, I was hired for my first nanny job by the mayor of Seattle ten years ago." He looked incredibly proud. "I was a janitor at the courthouse when we met. He liked the way I interacted with his kids. They were with him a lot after his wife left him. So, he gave me my first nanny job. And from there, I stayed in the business as each of my kids grew up."

He called them *his* kids, which is a lot better than them being called charges. "So you've got a knack with kids?"

"I took care of my younger brothers when I was younger, too. It's a gift," he said with a smile. "People don't usually think of men as *au pair*s, but I can do better with kids than lots of women. I think like one, I suppose. Fun is my number one thing. If my kids are having fun, smiling and laughing, then I've done my job."

"That's great." I liked that attitude. "Kids aren't meant to just behave and learn." I'd heard far too much from the other candidates I'd interviewed about teaching kids how to behave and making them learn all the time. None had talked about playing and letting them have fun.

I looked over his resume to see if he'd taken care of little girls before. "My daughter is three. Do you think you could deal with that?"

"Sure can," he said with certainty. "Little Miss Dana was two when I worked for the mayor. She wrapped me around her little finger, that's for sure." He sat back, then looked at me with a curious expression. "If you don't mind me asking, is the mother around?"

"My wife passed away from cervical cancer a year ago, Manly." I sighed, then went on, "I won't lie to you. I wanted to hire a female to take care of Tabby. She needs a female role model in her life."

He nodded. "I see." Then he snapped his fingers. "I've got a sister who could come around to be that female influence."

I didn't know if that would be enough. "I don't know."

"Sir, when I worked for the mayor, his wife had split. Those kids didn't have no mama." That proud look came back to his dark eyes. "I got my sister doing things with them, too. And that helped loads. You can count on me, sir. I'll help your little girl. My sister loves to dote on children."

The man seemed genuine, and Tabby would love his playful ways. "I tell you what, Manly, let me do this next interview, and then I'll make a decision. You're my top pick right now."

He stood up, clapping his hands. "That sounds amazing. You've got to interview the last candidate. I have all the confidence in the world you will be giving *me* a call, Doc."

"And why's that?" I asked as the next person couldn't be that bad.

"She's a kid, Doc. No business helping anyone raise a child, but thinks her college degree will help her take care of someone else's kid." He reached out to shake my hand. "So, I'll be talking to you soon, sir."

Laughing, the guy made me feel great. "I'm sure you will."

When he left, I heard him laughing his way down the hall, and his laughter made me smile. I liked his outgoing personality and knew he'd make Tabby's time away from me fun for her.

He'd left the door slightly ajar, and the next person stepped up to it. I took the last resume out of the file to find very little listed on it. When the door moved, a young woman came in. "Dr. Arlen?"

"That's me. Come on in." I looked at the name on top of the resume. "Kyla Rush."

She took a seat without offering to shake my hand, and her eyes were glued to the desk. "I prefer to be called Ky."

Socially awkward, I couldn't help but feel for her as I'd been the same way in my younger years. "Okay, Ky. It's nice to meet you."

Her eyes flashed to mine for only a fraction of a second. "You, too."

I put the resume down because the only thing on it was her education in early childhood development. "Do you like children, Ky?"

She nodded, making the loose bun on top of her head bounce a bit. The bun was thick; her hair was quite long. It was the same color as Jennifer Aniston's and shined in the light. "I do like them." Then she looked into my eyes, and I saw the green in her hazel eyes glisten. "I adore them, really. I did some babysitting for my cousins in my teens. It was then I decided to pursue a career revolving around kids."

"And what do you like doing with kids, Ky?" Something about the young woman struck me. She hardly wore any makeup. Her skin was creamy and natural. Her lips were a natural pink and her cheeks had a slight rose hue to them. She was a healthy young woman.

The way her eyes danced told me she truly enjoyed children. "I love playing with them and watching them when they learn something new. I love talking to them and listening to them tell me things. Kids fascinate me. Their brains are developing at such a rapid rate; it defies imagination. One day they can't speak a word, the next day they're saying *dada* or *mama*. It's just a great thing to witness. You know what I'm saying?"

"Yeah." I couldn't stop looking into her eyes. So much in them intrigued me! "Do you have any siblings, Ky?"

"No, sir. I'm an only child." She looked down again, and I fought a powerful urge to lean forward and take her by the chin to raise her face back up, so I could look into those eyes again.

She didn't have an ounce of real experience, and she wasn't going to be the right nanny for us. But something told me to give her a shot anyway. "Well, Ky, can I be honest with you?"

Her eyes came back to mine. "Yes, sir."

"I'd like my daughter's nanny to have some experience." I pushed the last page of Manly's resume toward her, showing her the many job assignments he'd had. "This is typical of the resumes I've seen in the last few days."

"I understand, sir." She squinted as she looked at the paper in front of her. "Um, can I ask you a question?"

"I suppose so." I didn't see the harm in answering something for her.

She looked at me again. "I noticed how happy the last guy who left here was. Is that because you've pretty much gone with hiring him?"

I nodded. "Yeah." I saw no reason to lie.

The way her eyes cut to the side and her chest rose and fell told me that was troubling to her. "Sir, I've got a way of reading people. This isn't my business, but I feel I should tell you this." She bit her lower lip before saying, "He's not the person you think he is. Did he tell you his homeless-ten-year-old-taking care of his brothers after his mother overdosed-story?"

"No." *What is she talking about?* "Did he tell you that?"

She nodded. "He did. And I didn't believe him. The woman before him knew him. I think he's been a sitter for a while, but I don't trust him. You should know that before hiring him. I know you're not hiring me, but please don't hire him."

What the hell?

4

KY

Two days went by after what I considered to be the worst interview anyone had done in a million years. So when my cell rang with a number I didn't recognize, I answered it, thinking it was some scam. "What?"

For a moment, I heard only silence, then a man asked, "Ky?"

His voice smooth, deep, and incredibly attractive, I knew who it was right away. "Dr. Arlen?"

"Yeah," he said with a chuckle. "It's me."

"Oh, sorry about that. I thought you were some scam caller." My cheeks were heating with embarrassment, and I sat on a crate in the back of the store, pausing from throwing out the trash.

"I took your advice about the man I was going to hire," he said.

Maybe I was wrong about the guy. "And?"

"And after a background check, I learned he's using an alias. On top of that, he's got a police record. He had charges dropped, but only because of this mayor he got to know while working at the courthouse. He had to do mandatory civil service for six months after being convicted of theft."

"I'm glad you checked him out," I said, nodding to myself as I got up to head back inside to get back to work. "So, did you find yourself a sitter?"

"I think I have," he said.

I figured it was the woman, Sally. "She's got a lot of experience. I hope she works out for you."

He seemed puzzled as he asked, "And when did all this experience occur, may I ask?"

"I don't know." I didn't understand the guy.

"Ky, I picked you," he said.

"What?"

"I picked you," he said again. "Would you like to come over to discuss your salary?"

My head felt light. "Am I dreaming?"

"No," he said with a laugh. "I'll send my driver to pick you up. What's the address?"

"I'm at work." I didn't know what to do. "Um, damn, I'm not sure what to do here."

"Where do you work?" he asked.

"Judy's Grocery," I said as I started heading inside. "You know what? I'm going to tell Judy I've got another job and don't need this one anymore. Right? I should do that, right?"

"You should." He laughed, then said, "Text me your address. I'll give you an hour to get home, and then I'll send my driver to pick you up and bring you here. We've got lots to talk about, and I can't wait for Tabby to meet you."

Suddenly it hit me like a brick. *I got the job!* "I'll do that! Thank you!"

The rest of that hour blurred by as I was beyond excited. And when a Lincoln pulled up in front of my apartment, I nearly passed out. The driver stood at the back door, holding it open for me. "Good afternoon, Miss Rush. I'm Steven, Dr. Arlen's driver. I understand you are the new governess."

"I guess I am." I got into the backseat, taking in all the luxury. "Wow."

"I know." He shut the door, returned to the driver's seat, and off we went.

I had no idea where we were going and texted Carla to let her know. After several minutes, we arrived in the more affluent part of town, and my jaw dropped just a little. The Lincoln then turned into a set of iron gates, and I texting Carla that I'd arrived at my destination and new home. I put the phone away as I looked around in wonder.

The mansion loomed ahead of us, and I couldn't take my eyes off of it. "Wow."

When the car came to a stop, the driver honked the horn, and the front door opened immediately. Another man came out to the car, opening the door for me. "Hello, Miss Rush. I'm Mr. Randolph, Dr. Arlen's butler. Please come with me."

Feeling as if I walked on air, I got out of the car, following the man who looked a lot like of Clark Gable. "I'm Ky."

"Okay, Ky," he said as he led me through one grand room after another. "This way, please. They're over here in Tabby's playroom."

"I'm going to need a map of this place," I said in a near-whisper as I'd already lost my way.

"I'll make you one." The man seemed helpful. "We want you to make this place your home."

"Oh yeah." I'd forgotten that I would live in this place now that I was the little girl's nanny.

When he opened one of the many doors along a long, wide corridor, I saw the man who interviewed me sitting on the floor as a little blonde-haired girl skipped around him in a circle, singing like a fairy princess. Dr. Arlen's ice-blue eyes found mine, and he smiled with that smile that had taken my breath away the first time I saw it. "Ky!" He reached out to take his daughter's hand. "Look, Tabby, this is Ky, your new babysitter."

Shyly, the girl ducked her head as she climbed onto her daddy's lap. I went to them, trying my best to get over my nerves. "Hi, Tabby."

Peering at me from under thick, dark lashes, she said not one word. But her father did. "She's a little shy. But she'll warm up to you."

Taking a deep breath, I tried to get my brain to work. Taking a seat on the floor, too, I sat cross-legged, just like he did. "Your home is beautiful, Dr. Arlen."

Another smile curved his chiseled, caramel-colored lips. "It's your home now, too, Ky. I'll show you to your suite in a little while, and then Steven will take you back to your place to retrieve your things. You can move in today. If that's okay."

"Yeah." I didn't know how to act. "Sure, Dr. Arlen."

"We can't have that," he said. "Call me Alex."

I nodded, not knowing how to react. "I feel so weird."

"I bet you do." He reached out and lightly patted my shoulder. "You'll get used to this."

Trying to ignore the odd sensation that ran through me at his brief touch, I hoped he was right. "I'll try."

"Okay, let's go over the ground rules," he said as his daughter buried her face in his broad chest. The man was all muscle. I couldn't recall ever seeing anyone as good-looking as him in real life before. I tried to keep myself from staring. "Rule number one, whenever you leave this house with my daughter, you let Steven drive you. He's a former Navy SEAL and one of our bodyguards. You will never leave this house with my daughter without him. Got it?"

Nodding, I assured him I understood, "Totes got it."

He moved one hand through his thick, wavy, dark hair, and I had to concentrate, so I didn't sigh at how sexy that was. "Okay. Rule number two, my daughter's happiness is essential to me. I don't want you to think that spending time holding her or doing things with her is spoiling her. She's the center of my life, and I always want her to know that."

"Center, happy, okay to hold her," I said. "Got it."

"No hitting her, ever," he added. "And no yelling at her. No cursing in front of her. Lots of hugs, lots of attention, and lots of praise when she does things."

It was then that I realized there wasn't a woman around—like a mom or wife. "Um, where's her mom?"

"Back in Spokane," he said as he smoothed his hand over his

daughter's silky, blonde hair. "In a cemetery. We lost her to cancer last year."

I put my hand over my mouth as my gasp threatened to escape. "I'm so sorry." Then I knew why he wanted his daughter to get so much attention and praise. He was trying his best to make up for the loss of her mother.

Looking at them as Tabby wound her arms around her dad's neck and they hugged each other, I realized that they suffered through so much.

"So you can understand why I want things the way I do for our child?" he asked softly.

"I can." I had to wipe the tear away from my eye that had escaped. "I'll be good to her; I swear to you."

"Good. That's all I ask." He reached out, pressing his hand on my shoulder again, and how I felt didn't make sense. He touched only my shoulder, yet my tummy went tight, and moisture blossomed in places it hadn't before.

I didn't like my reaction and tried to remember that this man was now my boss. I couldn't look at him with puppy dog eyes. Not that I'd ever looked at anyone like that, ever, but he was different.

Not only was he beyond hot, but he was sweet, too, and he smelled awesome. I had no idea anyone could smell that damn good, but Alex did. I wrestled my wandering mind back to business. "So, what's the pay, boss?"

His smile came back, and my heart skipped a beat. "Well, you're getting free room and board. That means you get to eat whatever you want here. And feel free to tell the chef what you like. His name's Rudy, and you'll find him in the kitchen most of the time. Plus, you get free maid service. Our head maid is Chloe; she'll take care of keeping your rooms cleaned."

"Rooms?" *You've got to be kidding me. I only needed the one.*

"Yes, I told you that I've set you up in a suite." He pointed up. "All the bedrooms are upstairs. And all of them are suites. They each have a living area, you know—like a living room. And then there's the bedroom. Each one is equipped with twin walk-in closets and a full bathroom. Yours has a balcony, too."

I didn't know what to think. "This is like totes unbelieve—you know?"

Laughing, he nodded. "Yeah. I wasn't always this well-to-do. I grew up in a small home with my parents and little brother. My wife had the money. She came from old money and inherited loads of it. And those loads now belong to Tabby and me. And speaking of money, your salary will be dispersed on Fridays by my accountant who comes by to pay everyone each week. I'm starting you off at two-thousand."

"Wow," I thought I'd only be getting maybe half that much. "Two-thousand a month? That's more than I expected."

"Then you're really going to be surprised," he said with a grin that made my panties wet. "It's two-thousand a week, Ky."

"Wait! What?" He had to be joking. "Are you messing with me?"

"Not at all." His laughter shook his chest, causing Tabby to pull her face from it.

Finally, she looked at me. "I'm, Tabby," she warbled.

"I'm, Ky." I liked the way her green eyes sparkled. "Do you like to play with dolls?"

She nodded. "Do you?"

"I do." I looked at the toys that were scattered around her playroom. "Do you think I can play with some of your toys with you?"

She nodded, then climbed off her father's lap. "I'll get you some."

As she walked away from us to get some toys, Alex looked at me, mouthing, "Thank you."

I had no idea why he would thank me for doing my job, but I mouthed back, "You're welcome." It was hard to keep from smiling.

His cell rang, and he got up, pulling it out of his pocket; he answered it, then walked away. And I turned my attention to Tabby who brought three dolls. "These are my favorites."

She handed one of them to me. It had dark hair and blue eyes. "Thank you. I like this one. What's her name?"

"You get to make that up, Ky." She sat right down on my lap, facing out as she cradled the other two dolls in her little arms. "My babies are Fiona and Fairy."

"Staying with the first letter of 'F', I'll call mine Felicity." I put mine in the crook of my arm. "Do you like your hair to be braided, Tabby?"

"I don't know," she said as she looked back at me. "What does that mean?"

"If we can find a hairbrush, I can show you." Her hair would look adorable in a couple of braids.

Alex came back, looking at his daughter on my lap. His eyes met mine. "She doesn't do that with anyone but me."

I felt like I'd done something wrong. "I'm sorry."

"No," he said as he shook his head. "I'm glad."

Tabby looked up at him. "Daddy, can Ky braid my hair?"

One dark brow cocked at me, and he asked, "Will you be gentle?"

"Of course." I put the baby doll down to show him, easing a section of her hair away from the rest and making a small braid. "See, no pulling of hair at all. I've got the tenderest head of anyone I know. I learned how to make pain-free braids a long time ago."

"Then braid away." He leaned over, running his hand through Tabby's hair. "I just don't want anything to ever hurt my baby girl."

She'd been hurt enough by losing her mother. The thought made my heart ache. "I'll never hurt her; I promise you."

"I'll be right over there while you two get to know each other." He walked away to take a seat on one of the chairs in the playroom. With his attention on his cell phone, I took a really good look at the man—and the effect he had on me was something I'd ever experienced.

From the dark waves of hair that flowed around his face to the slight slope of his narrow waist, everything about him did something for me. I had to learn fast not to let that show.

5
ALEX

Ky seemed to be settling in just fine. Two short weeks later, Tabby and Ky seemed inseparable.

When the two of them stopped by the hospital to visit me on my first day at work, I found myself smiling from ear to ear as soon as I spotted them.

I couldn't avoid my attraction to Ky. No matter how hard I tried, I couldn't deny it. But I managed to keep that magnetism under wraps. She was young, and on top of that, she worked for me. It was a no-no all the way around.

Tabby waved her arms as she looked at me, squealing, "Daddy! It's me, Tabby!"

As I went to them, another doctor came our way. "So this is Tabby." Reagan Dawson was introduced to me that morning, and I told her about my little girl.

Tabby jumped into my arms, and I presented her to Reagan. "Tabby, this is Reagan. She works with me."

Typical of my daughter, she buried her face in my chest. Reagan just smiled. "Well, it's nice to meet you, Tabby." Then she looked at Ky, who seemed taken aback for some reason. "And you must be the *au pair*."

Ky nodded. "I'm Ky."

"Nice to meet you, Ky," Reagan said. "I'm sure we'll see lots of each other."

Ky looked at me. "Why?" Her expression was a mix of emotions. But I was pretty sure I saw jealousy in the mix.

"Because we work together." Reagan looked at Ky with a smile, then held up her left hand. "Married."

What was that about? "Anyway, what has you girls out and about today?" I asked.

"Tabby wanted to see where you work," Ky told me. "And we wanted ice cream. She wants you to join us. I told her you probably couldn't."

A little break wouldn't hurt anything. "Come on, let's see what the cafeteria has."

Reagan shook her head. "Nope. The ice cream there is not that good. But go over a block south to New Release. It's a café, and it's got the best ice cream and burgers. It's lunch time. Take a break if you'd like to."

Ky's eyes went to the floor. "It's okay if you don't want to go."

"But I do," I said. "See ya later, Reagan."

Ky followed me as I carried Tabby and headed to the exit. We walked all the way out before she said, "She's pretty."

"Who is?" I stopped to let her catch up.

"The other doctor," Ky said. "I thought you and she were dating."

"Nope." It *was* jealousy in her pretty eyes. "I'm not on the market to date."

"Good," came her quick response. Then she went beet red. "I mean... good because you have a lot to get over."

Sure she did.

"Yes, I do." I wasn't ready to do any dating. But the attraction to Ky wasn't lessening any. And I couldn't help doing what I was about to do. "After lunch, you should take Tabby to your favorite salon to get her hair cut and get yours done, too. I'm treating you two to a day of beauty."

"You don't have to do that," Ky said.

Then Tabby raised her head. "Uh huh, 'cause I want to get my hair cut, Ky. Please?"

"Well, *you* can. I don't have to get anything done." Ky reached up to touch her ponytail.

"I'd like to see your hair down, Ky. Get it cut and get anything else done that you want. It's my treat." I wasn't taking no for an answer. "And if they have someone who does makeup, get that done, too, and buy whatever it is they use, so you can do it on your own."

"But," Ky tried to protest.

"But nothing. I'm taking you two out for dinner this evening to a nice place and want my girls to look pretty." I clamped my lips shut tight after realizing what I said.

Ky finally said, "Okay then."

I saw the café ahead and went that way, crossing the street. "Traffic's kind of bad here. Stay beside me, Ky."

She hurried to stay at my side as we crossed the busy street. When we got inside, the menu was written on a chalkboard behind the counter. "We've got a lot to choose from. Go ahead and tell her what you want, Ky."

"Oh, I'm okay. I don't need anything," she said.

That girl just had to be hungry. "Then I'll order for you." In the two weeks we'd spent together living under the same roof, I'd yet to see that girl eat something. Her curvy figure must've shamed her for some reason, but she looked like a million bucks. "A kid's meal with a cheeseburger and chocolate milk and two double cheeseburgers with fries and cream sodas for us."

Ky looked away, putting her arms around herself, trying to hide her midsection. "I can't eat all that."

"I bet you can." I handed Tabby to Ky to pay for the food. "Find us a table, please."

Taking Tabby, Ky went to a booth in the back. Grabbing a booster seat, she put Tabby in it on one side of the table, then took the seat across from her. As I approached them, I looked at Ky who'd put her arms around herself again. Sliding in next to Tabby,

I asked, "Why does it seem like you're insecure about your weight?"

Her eyes rolled. "Um, prob because I'm fat."

"You are not." It's terrible the way women think they have to weigh next to nothing to be attractive. "You're perfect, Ky."

"I am not. I've got thunder thighs. And," she looked down at her large chest. "Well, too much up top. And don't get me started on my butt. I can't find jeans that fit me right. If they fit my big butt, they don't fit my waist for some reason."

How could she not see those were her best assets? "You need a new mirror if you think anything is wrong with your body."

She looked up at me and her eyes met mine. "You've got muscles on top of muscles. So how can you think my body doesn't have anything wrong with it?"

"Women are supposed to be softer than men," Some women liked to have lots of muscle mass, and that was all well and good. I liked my women soft.

Not that Ky could ever be mine.

"Oh yeah?" Her smile, though slight, made my heart skip a beat.

"Yeah." I wanted to reach across that table and take her hands in mine and hold them tight. "You're really a great beauty, Ky."

"Yeah," Tabby agreed. "You really are beautiful, Ky."

Ky's cheeks went red, but she wasn't about to let the compliment train end there. "You're beautiful, too, Tabby."

Tabby kissed my cheek. "And you are very handsome, Daddy."

"Thank you, Princess." I looked over at Ky to see her eyes cast down again.

The waitress brought the food, and I picked up my burger, waiting for Ky to take a bite of hers first. She smiled as she caught me watching her. "What are you looking at?"

"The first bite of food I've ever seen you take." I waited and watched.

She took a giant bite. "Happy?" she said around her mouthful.

"Ecstatic." I looked at Tabby. "Now you, Tabs."

She bit into her burger. "So yummy."

I took a bite and found mine to be yummy, too. "I agree."

We ate quietly as the food was too good. And when I saw the last bite go down Ky's throat, I felt happiness for that simple thing. She was beginning to feel more at home with us.

I wanted her to feel that way more than anything I've wanted in a very long time.

6

KY

THE DAY HAD WORN little Tabby out after spending it at the children's museum. She was fast asleep, having her dinner earlier than usual. That meant Alex and I would be dining alone. And it kind of thrilled me that we'd get some time alone together.

I was a month into my new job, and Alex was two weeks into his. As I headed to the dining room, I ran ideas through my head on how to start a conversation with the man I always felt tongue-tied around. Well, most of the time. Sometimes I felt at ease. That was starting to happen more and more.

The only thing that wasn't fading was the strong attraction I had for him. He probably had no idea that the way he talked to me and sometimes touched me made me feel like he might like me even more than I was sure he already did.

I knew he liked me for his daughter's sake. She and I got along like peas and carrots. But I hated myself for even thinking a man like him would actually be attracted me. He probably thought of me as a kid. Right off, he didn't like the way I looked; that's why he paid for me to get a nearly complete makeover.

That day after eating lunch together, Tabby and I went to a salon that Carla told me was the bomb. With Alex's credit card in hand, the ladies at that salon went gaga over Tabby and me. A few hundred dollars later, we emerged from the salon with gorgeous curls, and I had some highlights—a thing I never dared before.

The owner of the salon took before and after pictures of me and asked if she could use them on her website. I suppose my transformation was somewhat miraculous. So I gave her the go-ahead.

I should've gotten a pic of Alex's face when he came home that night. His eyes went wide, and he scanned my entire body, then he let out a whistle that made me blush.

He couldn't have been faking that expression.

Never had I seen anything like what I saw in Alex's eyes that night as I stood there under the chandelier in the foyer. They glistened—and then smoldered—making my knees go weak.

Avoiding asking myself what I was doing, I'd gotten myself cleaned up nicely after putting Tabby to bed. I put on a dress that I picked up while we were out that day. Some two-inch heels adorned my feet. I couldn't walk in anything higher than that. My hair was down my back; I straightened it, not having the time to curl it the way they had at the salon. My makeup was on point, too. I was getting good at applying it just right.

I hadn't seen Carla in a month. She would be blown away. That's my excuse as to why I got all dolled-up. After dinner, I planned to see my old friends and roomies. It was Friday, and the girls usually had a few drinks while watching Vampire Diaries.

Although not one to participate in the drinking part of the evening, I might try one cocktail this time. I'd begun feeling a lot more like a grownup instead of the kid I always thought of myself as. And I hoped Alex would start to look at me that way, too.

Why, I didn't know. It was bad form to date the person you work for. That's what everyone at the employment agency said. At the grocery store where I worked, employees were forbidden to date each other.

But I couldn't seem to control my actions at times. Like this evening where I purposely got dressed up just to see my boss's response. I didn't know what got into me.

Strolling into the dining room, I heard Alex's voice coming from the kitchen on the other side of it, "And some red wine, too, Rudy. I'm off this weekend and want to get this relaxation started."

Just as I was about to take a seat, Alex came in, his eyes going wide and running up and down my body. "You look..." he stopped talking and just looked at me. "Amazing."

I ran my hand down my side, letting it rest on my hip. The dress had a vintage look: simple, brown, and just above my knees. The V-neckline plunged lower than anything I'd ever worn before. But it still wasn't anywhere near as daring as the things my roomies would wear. "You like?"

He nodded, then came over to me, pulling my chair out, then pushing it back in. I felt his body heat beside me.

"Your text said Tabby had gone to sleep already. If that's the case, then we shouldn't mess up this larger dining area. Shall we go to the lounge for dinner? It's smaller, less for the staff to clean up."

"If you'd like." I'd never been in the lounge. There were so many rooms I'd never seen in this mansion.

When he took my hand and placed it in the crook of his arm, I felt a shiver run through me. "I would like that very much." He led me to the kitchen first. "Rudy, we'll be dining in the lounge this evening."

"Yes, sir," the chef said, then went back to work.

Off we went to the lounge, and when Alex pushed open the door, I thought I was in a small tavern. An ornate wooden bar ran along the far wall. When he flipped a switch, the lights above it came on, making the tons of glass bottles filled with different alcohols glisten.

Three small tables were placed around the dimly lit room. He went to one, pulled out a chair and moved me into it. Then he took the chair across from me. "Looks like you've made plans for tonight."

"I'm going to see my old roommates after dinner." A flicker of disappointment crossed his icy blue eyes. "Unless you need me to stay home. I didn't even think to ask if you had plans. How rude of me. I won't go. It's not a big deal." I felt like an idiot for not asking him.

"No. You can go, Ky." He looked up as one of the chef's assistants came in with a bottle of wine and two glasses, along with a cheeseboard. "Thank you, Delia."

She filled the glasses with a smile, then left us alone again. I took a sip of the wine. My nerves were unsteady, and I needed something to help calm them. "Okay, I'll go then. If you have nothing to do tonight."

Silent, he looked at me as if he wanted to say something more, then just smiled. "I have no plans, Ky. Just a quiet evening at home."

It almost sounded like he'd be lonely. He wouldn't even have Tabby to hang out with since she was in bed already. "What will you do here, all alone?"

Shrugging, he said, "Probably watch some television."

"That's all we were going to do to." I didn't want to leave him home by himself for some reason. The thought of him sitting alone, watching TV made me feel sort of sad. "How about I stay home and watch something with you? I'll look up some fun cocktail recipes and make something. You've got just about everything a bartender could possibly need. It'll be fun. Have you ever watched Vampire Diaries?"

Shaking his head, his soft voice sent chills through me, "No. You sure you want to spend your Friday night with me?"

"Yeah." The truth was, I was getting pretty excited about it. "I wanted to find out how you like your new job anyway." I picked up a piece of cheese to nibble on and found him smiling at me.

"I like my new job just fine." He mirrored me, picking up a chunk of cheese, too. "And I like that you're finally eating in front of me without coaxing."

My cheeks heated with shame. "To be honest, I was starving myself for reasons unknown. That's dumb—and immature, childish, etcetera."

"You were overwhelmed by everything." He patted the back of

my hand that I rested on the table near my glass of wine. "You never expected to get this job."

"No, I did not." Everything felt like a shock to me, including this visceral attraction I had for him. "I'm getting used to things now. My appetite has come back."

"I'm glad." His hand stayed on mine. "And how do you like taking care of Tabby? Be honest. It can't be as great as you make it seem to be."

"It *is* that great." I always had a lot of fun with the little girl. "I've fallen in love with your daughter, Alex. She's such a great kid. I wake up, ready to see her. It's crazy, but I do. And when I put her to bed early tonight because she was so worn out, I actually missed her company afterward." I looked him directly in his gorgeous eyes. "Thank you for this opportunity. I had no idea I could feel this way."

"Yeah, me neither." He took a drink of his wine. "So, tell me about yourself, Ky."

"There's not much to tell." I hadn't done much with my personal life. "I've worked at the grocery store since I was sixteen. I went to a community college after graduating from high school. I sold my car to pay for my classes instead of getting into debt with student loans."

"Smart move." He finally took his hand off mine. "I went into the Navy. That's who paid for my medical degree. My father urged me to join after graduation from high school. I had gotten into some bad habits, drinking, smoking pot. He figured that it might benefit me, and it did. Funny how he and the rest of my family are making money from selling pot nowadays."

"They do? Where?"

"Colorado. Where it's legal." He cocked his head as if thinking about something. "When I take Tabby to see them next month, you'll meet them."

He's taking me to meet his parents?
Of course, he is. You work for him, taking care of his kid, you fool!

"That'll be cool." I took a sip of wine. "What was it like in the Navy? I've always wondered about that. Were you ever in a battle?"

"I saw some action." He unbuttoned his white shirt, making my breath catch in my throat. His muscular pec began to peek out, and then he exposed it completely, showing me an incredible tattoo of an anchor. "I got this in Thailand to commemorate those days."

My pussy got wet just by looking at that massive pec. *Can I touch it?* "That must've been something."

"It was." He left his shirt open and picked up the wine glass. My eyes went to his bicep as it flexed with the action. "Sometimes I have nightmares that I never left the military, and this life is nothing more than a delusion." He put the glass down. "And when Rachelle got sick, then died, I prayed that was nothing more than a dream."

"But you've stayed rational for your daughter."

Nodding, he looked down. "Yeah. She's all I've got."

He deserves more. So much more.

7

ALEX

SITTING THERE with my shirt open in front of Ky wasn't a thing I planned on doing. I couldn't even blame the wine since I'd only taken a couple of sips before doing it.

Feeling a little embarrassed, I buttoned up my shirt, and I was glad to see the meal being served as Delia came in with our plates. "Steak and lobster."

Ky was taken aback. "Oh, wow!"

Her happy expression did things to my heart. "I called Rudy this afternoon, thinking you'd like this."

She looked at me with even more astonishment. "You did this for *me*?" Her hand on her chest had me taking a quick glance at the cleavage she'd never displayed before. It made my mouth water.

"Yes." I wanted something extravagant for Ky's dinner and made the call. "I figured you hadn't had a lot of surf and turf in your life."

"I have not." She eyed the plate hungrily. "Thank you so much, Alex."

It made me happy to see her digging into her food. We ate every last bit, then went to the media room to watch some television. Ky took the baby monitor out of the pocket of her dress, placing it on the table next to the chair she'd taken.

"You've got a natural instinct with children, Ky. I never thought about carrying around a baby monitor with me. Whenever Tabby went to sleep, I found myself trapped in her room to hear her if she woke up. I've slept more nights on that girl's floor than I care to think about."

"Well, good thing I'm here now." She saw the remote on the table and reached out to get it. The curve of her hip caught my eye when she leaned over to hand it to me as I took the chair next to hers. "Here you go."

"So, Vampire Diaries, huh?" I turned on the huge flat screen that hung on the wall. "Is that on Netflix?"

"Yes." She took her heels off, then curled her legs under herself, getting comfy. "Oh, I almost forgot to pour us my apple martinis." She jumped up to go to the tray she'd brought. Before leaving the lounge, she'd mixed up a batch of the cocktail and had grabbed a couple of martini glasses, too.

I found the show she wanted and asked, "Can I start it from the beginning?"

"Of course." She came back, handing me a glass. "Here you are."

I took a sip. "Mm. Apple-ish."

"Yes, it is." She took her seat again, and I looked at her with desire. I'd never gotten total control over my appeal for her and began to wonder if I ever would.

After binge-watching three episodes, I saw Ky beginning to nod off, and I called it a night. We walked upstairs together, and it almost felt like we'd gone on a date. "I had fun tonight, Ky."

"Me, too." She stopped in front of the door to her suite with a smile. "I'm glad I stayed home."

"Me, too." The urge to kiss her nearly overwhelmed me as we stood there, just outside of her bedroom. I imagined me taking her inside and laying her down on the bed, peeling her clothes away from her curvy body. "Good night then."

"Good night." She went into her room, softly closing her door, and I looked down to see my cock growing inside my jeans. "Shit."

Heading to my room a few doors down, I went to take a hot shower. I hadn't self-pleasured myself in a while, and my balls begun to ache. The need to release along with my built-up desire for Ky had me ditching my clothes in record time and lathering up my hands in the shower for a steamy fantasy starring Ky.

Her smooth skin under my hands, her lips pouty and full, the feel of her nails grazing down my back—it all made chill bumps rise on my flesh.

I could still smell her sweet scent as I touched myself, pretending it was her. "Ky, my sweet little Ky, what you do to me is insane."

Tilting her face up to mine, her lips parted, then I took them with a slow, burning kiss that made my cock even harder. Her tongue moved around mine, tempting me to kiss her more.

Clinging to her naked body, I forced my tongue deeper into her mouth, testing her gag reflex, hoping she'd suck my cock. She took the hint, pulling her mouth away from mine, and then sliding her body down until she landed on her knees, her beautiful face on the same level as my erection.

Pursing her lips, she kissed the tip of the massive serpent that yearned for her attention. Her soft hands glided down my shaft, then back up again. Pressing her lips to the tip once more, she opened them, licking it over and over as she stroked me.

I had to lean back on the warm tiled wall of the shower, letting the water cascade over my face as she licked me into a frenzy of desire, lust, and passion. "Suck me off, baby."

Her mouth opened wide to let me in. The heat of it enveloped my hard cock, then she moved her head forward until I felt the back of her throat touching the head of my pulsing appendage.

"Deeper, baby. Take me deeper." I ran my hands through her hair, tangling them in as I moved her head to suit me. "Suck me, baby."

Her mouth felt magical as I moved her head back and forth. Every part of my body was on fire for her. I wanted to bury my cock deep in her soaked pussy so badly, but first, she'd taste my seed, swallow it all, and then beg me for more.

Moving one hand a bit, she cupped my balls, tenderly

massaging them as she sucked my cock with equal gentleness. Her pretty head looked fantastic as it bobbed in front of me.

My breathing grew ragged as I watched her take me all in. Then my cock jerked in her mouth, and I groaned as I ejaculated in it. She drank it all before pulling her mouth off me, leaving me a helpless puddle of the man I'd been. "Alex, I want you inside of me now."

"Oh, yeah!" I took her by the shoulders, turning her around and then pushing her down until she was on all fours. Then I rammed my hard dick into her from behind, making her whimper.

I fucked her hard and fast. Her hard breaths and soft moans of pleasure filled my ears. Her sweet voice interjected, "Fuck me, Alex. Please fuck me harder."

Going harder, I heard the slapping of our flesh as I showed her who she belonged to. "You're mine, Ky. Only mine."

"Yes," she hissed. "Yours. I am yours, Alex. Only yours."

Moving faster and harder, I felt her insides begin to quake around my cock, then I let her have it as she climaxed, and I did, too. "Mine!"

Panting, I leaned my head on the shower wall, my body spent. It was good, but not what I knew it could be with the actual woman. A woman who was right under my roof—only a feet away from me.

Grabbing a towel, I dried off, then went to bed, not bothering to put on pajamas. If Tabby woke up, Ky would tend to her.

Ky had come into my home and life and become the closest thing to a mother my daughter ever had. Rachelle hadn't been able to do much since she'd gotten sick only months after Tabby was born. She couldn't be a mother to her or a wife to me.

As I lay in my bed, one I never shared with my wife, I thought about the reality of my situation. I hadn't had sex with a woman in nearly three years.

Was my attraction to Ky only because she was the first women to be around me for any real length of time? Or was it a legitimate magnetism?

Ky was wonderful. She was like an angel sent from Heaven for both me and Tabby. Maybe it wasn't right for me to have sexual fantasies about the young woman. I didn't know for sure—but I felt helpless to stop them.

That hadn't been my first fantasy about Ky. I had plenty of them since she'd come to work for me. And I had many dreams featuring her, too—dreams where she and I weren't employer and employee, but much more.

Can Ky ever be what she is to me in my dreams? Do I even have the right to ask her for more than she's already given?

Thirteen years separated us. Were there too many years to move on my attraction? Was it right of me to make a play for the young woman when she worked for me?

Something told me it wasn't. I needed some space from her for a while. I needed to leave, to get away and clear my head.

It had been so damn long since I lived with a woman. And living with Rachelle hadn't been the same as living with a wife.

I'm starved for affection. That must be it.

It wasn't right to seek it from the young woman who took care of my little girl, either. I needed to find that elsewhere.

Don't I?

So what if Ky seemed like the perfect woman? She was young, gorgeous, and innocent. At least she seemed to be innocent. She didn't act like most women her age. She never flirted, never showed off more skin than necessary.

Ky has to be a virgin.

Then my cock twitched with the thought. *There's a virgin in your home, buddy. We should definitely tap that.*

Pulling the blanket up, I gave my meddling appendage a scowling glare. "How dare you talk about Ky that way. She's not some tramp you know."

And now I'm talking to myself out loud.

I put the blanket down, willing my cock to stop torturing me. Ky being a virgin shouldn't have mattered to me anyway.

She offered no information on her sex life. She'd never come-on to me. So why was I entertaining the thought that she might be an innocent young woman who I could ravage and ruin for other men, making her mine and mine alone?

When did I become such an animal?

I really needed to get out of town for a while. Putting some space between us would be the right thing to do. That's all I needed: some space and time to get myself back under control.

At this rate, I'd be banging on Ky's door in no time, begging her to let me bury my cock in her sweet, innocent pussy.

Good Lord, Alex!

8

KY

When I woke up the next morning, I found Tabby's bed empty, which scared me to death. Running to bang on Alex's door, I found the maid in his room, cleaning it. "Do you know where Alex and Tabby are?"

"They left early this morning. I saw them when I came in," Bernadette told me. "He said they're going to Spokane to see the baby's grandparents." She pulled something out of the pocket of her apron. "He said to give this to you."

I took the white envelope out of her hand, then went back to my suite, opening it as I walked away. The note said Alex had made a quick decision to take Tabby to see his wife's parents. They'd be back on Sunday night. I had the weekend off and could use any of the cars I wanted to while they were gone.

The night before had been so nice that I thought we might do more things together that weekend.

Going to sit on the sofa in the living area of my suite, I decided to go out with my friends that night. I had to get my mind off Alex. And I already missed Tabby.

Calling up Carla, I tried to get back into my own life. "You're up early," she answered my call.

"Yeah," I said. "You want to hang out today and maybe go out tonight?"

"Whoa! Am I dreaming?" she asked with shock in her voice. "You want to go out?"

"Yes. My boss took his daughter to see her grandparents for the weekend, and I'm bored. I've never gone out with you girls. Maybe it's time. It'll be my treat. We can even go to that salon and get them to gussy us up."

"Who is this?" Carla asked as she laughed. "And where has my friend gone?"

"You just be ready. I'll pick you up shortly."

"You bought a car?"

"No, but my boss said I can use one of his while they're out of town. I guess he gave the driver the weekend off, too." I couldn't help but feel Alex left because of our time spent together. *Was he was afraid of me or something?*

Maybe he caught me looking at him with stars in my eyes when I was sure he wouldn't catch me. Maybe he didn't know how to tell me he didn't want anything sexual? Maybe he wanted to fire me?

"Cool, pick a fast one," Carla said with a sinister tone to her voice.

"I won't be misusing Alex's car, Carla. And all I can have is one drink tonight since I'll be driving." I thought better of it and added, "Scratch that. I won't be drinking at all since I'll be driving."

"Now, you sound like the Ky I knew before she became a governess." The sigh she made told me she was disappointed. "How about we take a cab, and we can all drink then? I want you to have some fun, girl. For a minute, you sounded like you were going to."

She was right. I'd always been so conscientious. "Okay. I'll drive over, and we can take the car to shop and get our hair and makeup done, then we'll leave the car at the apartment when we go out. See, still having fun, but doing it responsibly."

"Oh, man, what an old lady you are, Ky," she groaned. "Just get over here."

I honestly never cared when someone called me an old lady.

Peer pressure wasn't a thing to me. My mother said I had an old soul. Whatever it was, I knew better than to get myself into trouble.

At least before I met Alex. Now it seemed I'd scared him away with my attraction to him. And I tried so damn hard not to let it show. I had to find a guy to take Alex off my mind.

I'd never been on the hunt for a guy before. This was new territory. But I had this feeling that if I had another man, I'd stop pining away for my boss. I needed to stop that ASAP or I might lose my job. And I loved my job.

After making a vow to myself that I'd, at the very least, kiss some guy that night, I felt a little sick about it. But I had to do something. The sexual tension I felt whenever Alex was around was getting to me.

I had a fantasy about Alex during the night that had me wanting to walk over to his room and take him like a siren in the night. If I didn't do something, I would def end up sneaking into the man's bed, and then what?

You'd get a righteous fucking is what would happen.

Shaking my head, I gathered my things, then headed to the garage. I knew better than to believe my inner whore who only recently reared her ugly head.

Alex wouldn't give me a righteous fucking. He'd tell me to leave his room, his home, his daughter, and fire me. And he'd be right to do so.

As I walked through the house, it seemed Alex had let everyone but one maid have the weekend off. I went out to the garage and ogled the five cars there. He had even more than these. Six were still in Spokane.

He wasn't a collector of cars though—his wife was. And she'd been the one to pick out the baby blue Mercury Cougar in the furthest stall.

I looked upward. "So, Rachelle, would it be alright if I drove your little beauty over there?"

No thunder boomed, no lightning struck, so that meant she'd

be fine with it. I took the keys off the board that hung on the wall, then went to get into the nearly brand-new car.

It was three years old, but only had four hundred miles on the odometer. The buttery-smooth leather smelled new, too. I pictured Rachelle driving it.

Alex didn't have pictures of his wife all over the place, but three were in Tabby's bedroom. One with Tabby when she was a newborn. One with Alex and Tabby when she was a little older, and one of Rachelle alone and pregnant.

Tabby looked more like her mother: long blonde hair, emerald green eyes, and just the lightest dusting of freckles across both their noses made them look like doppelgängers.

My mind wandered to a place where Alex and I had a daughter, and she looked like him: icy blue eyes, dark wavy hair, and beautiful.

Shaking my head to clear it, I pushed the button to open the garage door and get my day started. It was time to let Alex and Tabby go for a while.

Carla and I had one hell of a day, shopping, primping, then climbing into a cab to head to a club she liked to frequent. We met the other girls there, and it was a lot of fun.

We danced in a crowd to some hard-pounding beat, then I felt a hand on my ass and spun around to find some dude smiling at me. His arms as thin as his legs, he wasn't my type.

I didn't say a thing to him, just danced away, leaving him to find another girl to fondle. Carla had found some chick to grind on, and I ended up dancing behind them, feeling out of place.

A drink might help me loosen up.

I walked to the bar and ordered a seven and seven. I didn't know what that was, but I heard Carla order that before. It was a pleasant surprise; it tasted like 7 Up. I downed a quarter of it pretty quickly as I'd gotten overheated with all the dancing and the cumulative warmth of all the moving bodies.

Finding a place away from the dance floor, I soon became the focus of one man. An older man: nice-looking, fit, buff. He came my way, a short glass with a dark liquid in it in his hand. "Hi. I haven't seen you around before. New in town?"

I shook my head. "Nope. I've lived here all my life. Just new to the clubbing world is all."

His dark eyes ran over me, making me feel like running away, but I stayed where I was. "New to clubbing? How old are you, baby?"

I didn't much like him calling me that. That's what Alex called me in my fantasies about him. "Twenty-two. And you?"

"Thirty-three." He grinned. "Is that too old for you, baby?"

I shifted my weight to my other foot; my feet were hurting since Carla made me buy three-inch heels. I shook my head. "No, that's not too old." I was interested in Alex who was thirty-five after all. "My mother says I'm an old soul."

"Whatever that means," he said as he looked away from me at another girl who walked by.

"Wow," I said as I followed his gaze. "You should go after her."

He looked back at me. "Nah. What I see here is better."

I didn't much care for the way he said things. "Look, I'm not interested. Just go."

With wide eyes, he turned and left me. And I watched him go, thankfully. Sure, I made a vow to at least kiss a guy, but I wasn't about to be treated like a piece of meat.

I took a seat on a nearby barstool and saw another guy approaching. "Hey, sexy."

I extended my hand. "Name's Ky, not sexy. And you are?"

"Horny," he said with a grin as he took my hand in his, not bothering to shake it the way I meant him to. "Care to join me in the men's room for a quickie?"

"Do girls actually fall for that line?" I tugged my hand out of his.

"All the time." His hand ran through the thick mop of dark hair on his head as his hazel eyes sparkled while he looked me over. "And you are one Grade A cut of pussy. I want all up in that."

Oh, hell no!

"I've got to get the hell out of here." I got up to leave, putting my cocktail on the bar.

His hand caught my wrist before I could get away. "Don't be like that." He pulled my hand down until I could feel the bulge in his pants. "You'll like what I got, I promise."

Yanking my hand back, I quickly slapped him in the face before walking out of the club. Carla had seen it all and came out behind me. "What did that guy say to you, Ky?"

"Just normal jackass shit." I was furious and wanted to get the hell away from there. "This place is a cesspool."

Carla laughed. "What the heck is a cesspool, Ky?"

"You know, like a sewer, Carla. How can you go to places like this?" How she could stomach people talking to her the way I'd been spoken to?

"Look, I know this place is a little raunchy," she admitted as a cab pulled up. "Come on. We'll go somewhere more your style."

I didn't want to go anywhere else. But I made a vow to myself, and we went to another club.

Maybe someone could fill my sexual void and get Alex out of my mind.

9

ALEX

SITTING in the back of the Lincoln with Tabby as Steven drove us home from the airport late Sunday night, I couldn't shake the feeling I had. Being around Rachelle's parents never failed to set me off.

Being around them without my wife was always peculiar. It made me feel empty again. Alone again. I'd thought I'd left some of that behind with Ky being around. Going back to Spokane was a mistake. But I'd always have to do it, so Tabby could see her grandparents.

I made them a promise before I left Spokane to bring her back as much as I could. But when I made that promise, I had no idea how tough it would be to go back.

Visiting Rachelle's grave wasn't easy either. When Gabby put the flowers we'd brought onto the grave, I nearly cried. I just wanted it over with already.

There had to be more for me. This couldn't be it.

We pulled to a stop in front of our home, and I got out. Tabby had fallen asleep in her car seat, and I lifted her out of it, then carried her inside. When I walked down the hall, passing the door to Ky's suite, it opened, and there she stood in a pink nightgown.

"Oh!" Ky exclaimed and then hastily shut the door. "You're back!"

With only a glimpse, I noticed how her nipples pressed against the satin fabric and the way her thighs were as creamy as her face. "Yeah, we're home."

And so is my hard-on for you.

Carrying one's daughter to bed while an erection was coming on wasn't comfortable.

Quickly, I put Tabby into bed, taking off her shoes, then tucking her in snugly. I turned on the baby monitor before leaving her and went back to the hallway.

Standing there for a long time, I fought myself from going to Ky's door. But I lost the battle and knocked on it. She opened it, this time wearing a white terrycloth robe that hid everything from my prying eyes. "Yes, Alex?"

"Can we talk for a minute?" I asked her but didn't know why.

"Sure." She backed up. "Come in." Taking a seat on the loveseat, she watched me sit down on the sofa. "You seem out of sorts."

"I am." She already could tell when I wasn't myself? "It's seeing Rachelle's parents. They make me feel bizarre. Her mother asks me way too often how I'm doing without Rachelle."

"And what do you tell her?" Ky asked as she pulled her robe tighter around her.

"That I'm doing fine. It isn't what she wants to hear. She doesn't believe me. She wants to see me shed tears. I swear she does. Why would she continuously point out things like Tabby never knowing her mother if she wasn't trying to get me to cry?"

Nodding, Ky was sympathetic. "Maybe she just wants company in her sorrow?"

How could Ky guess such a thing about a person she had never even met? "Rachelle's father refuses to speak much about her. When he does, he mentions her as if she's still alive."

"So he's pushing sorrow to the side, not thinking of her as departed, but merely not there at the moment." Ky moved around in the chair, pulling her bare feet under her while making sure the robe kept her covered.

She should lose the robe entirely. Those perky tits underneath the thin satin was all I cared about at that moment.

Then I chastised myself for thinking that way. I left for the precise reason that I had to get her out of my mind. But all I did was think about her and what she was doing. "So, what did you do while we were away, Ky?"

"Nothing." She looked at me with determined eyes. "I think you need to talk about this visit some more, Alex. You don't look right. You've got dark circles underneath your eyes. Did you sleep well?"

"No." They put Tabby and me up in Rachelle's childhood bedroom. "I swear that woman was baiting me at every turn. She put us in my wife's old bedroom—it's like a shrine. There are pictures of her all over the room: her as a high school cheerleader, a college graduate, even our wedding photo."

Ky's eyes went wide. "Oh, man. I bet you had dreams about her the whole time."

"One would think that." One would've been wrong. I dreamt of Ky instead.

"So, you must've stayed awake to stop the dreams from continuing," she gathered.

"I did keep waking up." She was right about that part.

However, I wanted to stop the dreams about Ky. It seemed wrong to be in my departed wife's old room dreaming erotically as our daughter slept a few feet away from me. The whole idea of getting Ky off my mind hadn't worked at all.

"Maybe you shouldn't have done that, Alex," Ky commented. "Maybe you should dream about her?"

"And what good is that?" I really wanted to know, but I wasn't talking about Rachelle; I was talking about Ky.

"Live out time with her," she said. "Even if it's only in a dream, live in that moment with her."

In a way she was right. I could only have Ky in my dreams

anyway. I might as well stop fighting it and enjoy it. But while sleeping in a room with my kid? No way.

"Um, the dreams were a bit explicit. Not with Tabby in the same room."

"Oh," she finally understood. "But now that you're home and have privacy, allow yourself that time with your wife."

Ky had no idea how things had gotten with my wife. "Um. Our marriage wasn't the same after Tabby was born. Rachelle came down with ovarian cancer a few months after the birth... If I share too much, just tell me to stop."

"'Kay," she said with a serious expression.

"Anyway, the last time we had sex was a week before Tabby was born." I let that sink in.

What I saw on Ky's face made me feel awful. There was so much sadness on her face; I truly was pathetic. "So it's been years?"

I nodded. "There's never been anyone else after Rachelle."

"That must be rough." She looked at the floor. "You must've really loved her."

"I did." I was a devoted husband until the end. But the end had come for us long ago. I didn't have to hold onto my commitment to her. "As much as I loved her, I'm learning to let it go. I can't hold onto her forever. She was sick for a long time. To see her out of misery was all I wanted. I gladly let her go so she could escape the pain."

"Noble," Ky observed. "Courageous even."

As strong as it sounded, I was anything but that. "No. I was as tired as Rachelle was of all the pain. When she passed on, a lot of responsibility fell away. A weight lifted off my shoulders. And I kicked myself for feeling that way for a while."

"I'm sure seeing her in pain was a burden, Alex." *How did she know that?*

Ky was young and had never dealt with things like that. "You're wise beyond your years. Has anyone ever told you that, Ky?"

"My mother calls me an old soul." She smiled. "And I have this ability to empathize with others, especially if I feel close to them."

"So you feel close to me then?" I asked. I wanted her to feel that way, but then again, it wasn't appropriate.

"I suppose living here with you guys makes me feel that way." She looked off to the side. "Can I ask you something?"

"Yes." So long it wasn't a question of me being attracted to her. What would I say about that? The girl had me saying things I normally wouldn't.

"Are you feeling gloomy and concerned?" she asked. "That's what I feel coming off you right now."

"Yes." She must've thought it was over my wife, but it wasn't over Rachelle, it was over her.

I was sad because all I wanted was to take this woman in my arms and love her. And I was worried because I knew it wasn't appropriate and had no idea how much longer I could hold myself back from doing the things I dreamt and fantasized about.

"You don't need to worry, Alex." She looked at me with kindness in her hazel eyes. "Tabby will be okay. And one day you will, too. It's okay to feel sad. You lost your one true love after all."

The thing was, I had thought of Rachelle as my one true love, but now I didn't anymore. I could see myself with Ky. I could see a future with her. How would this work? What would Ky do if I told her that?

"I hope you're right, Ky." I didn't know what else to say. "So, you didn't just lie around the house. Tell me what you did over the weekend."

She looked slightly uneasy then finally said, "I've never went out and partied the way others do. You know, clubbing."

"So you went clubbing?" I felt a twinge of jealousy.

"Yeah." She wrinkled her nose. "It's not for me."

Good.

10

KY

"You certainly don't seem like the clubbing type," Alex said as he grinned. "And to be honest, I'm glad."

What does he mean he was glad? Because he didn't want some loose tramp watching over his daughter? "Yeah, I figured you'd say that."

He looked sheepish before asking, "So did a guy capture your attention? Or several?"

My cheeks got hot with humiliation thinking about the men I'd met. "Um... to be honest none of them really took my attention. I did have some, for lack of a better word, *come on* to me. Some were more aggressive than others."

"How?" he asked with a frown.

He seems jealous. How he could feel jealous when he still loved his deceased wife? I had to be misreading him. "This one guy touched my butt without even seeing my face first. That was weird."

"And remarkably uncalled-for," he said. "I hope you let him know that was not okay."

"I didn't say anything." The music was so loud he wouldn't have heard me anyway. "But I danced away from him."

"At least you got away." He looked somewhat relieved. "I hope that was the worst of it for you."

"No." I shudder to recall the feel of that lump in another guy's pants.

"There's more?" Alex looked pissed. "Tell me."

Why would he be mad?

Alex did not see me as anything but his kid's nanny. *Try to understand that and stop thinking he wants me for anything other than that.* "Well, this one guy came up to me while I sat at the bar alone."

"Why were you alone?" Alex asked with concern. "Didn't you go with friends? Please don't tell me you went out alone. Do you know how risky that could be, Ky?"

"I went out with my friend, Carla." Concern was etched in his voice. "After I got away from the butt-grabber, I wanted to get out of the crowd. So I went to get a drink at the bar. I ordered what Carla had before, a seven and seven."

He frowned again. "How many of those did you drink?"

"Um... About a quarter of one drink." I smiled. Alex seemed so alarmed; it made me feel wiggly inside. "Anyway, this one older guy approached me. Thirty-three, he said he was and asked me how old I was. When I replied, he asked if he's too old for me."

"And you said?" Alex asked with curiosity.

"I said no." His face changed to one of concern.

"So the man did what?"

"He checked out another girl who walked by, and I told him he should go after her." He pissed me off when he did that, and my ideas of giving my first kiss to him dissipated. Alex didn't need to hear that part.

Nodding, he said, "Sorry, you had a dreadful time." He didn't look sorry though.

"Then this other guy really made me mad when he came up to me, talking to me like he knew me, asking me to go to the bathroom with him for a quickie." I didn't say anything else, because Alex jumped up out of his seat.

Fury filled his handsome face. "He did *what*?"

"I said no." I couldn't wipe the smile off my face. He was *actually* jealous! "When I tried to walk away, he grabbed my hand."

Alex shook with rage. "He did *what*?" he repeated louder.

His anger was adorable. "He grabbed my hand and pressed it against his erection. It was vulgar."

It was too much for him. Alex exploded, "That son-of-a-bitch! I hope you called the cops on him." He stood in front of me, towering over me.

The scent of his cologne combined with the spicy smell of perspiration that had formed on him. And when I answered, "No," he looked at me like I'd just stabbed him in the heart.

His face fell. "Don't tell me you fell for that, Ky."

"Of course, not." Relief flooded his face. "I yanked my hand back and slapped him, then left the place and vowed never to go back."

"That's good." He walked to sit back down. "So you came home after that?"

"No, we went to one more club." Now that one wasn't as bad.

Alex's face had fallen again. "What happened there? Did you find someone?"

I shook my head. "No. It was a piano bar. We sang along with everyone else, and I had fun."

"No one turned your head?" he asked as he sat back down. He might be okay now that he knew I hadn't hooked up with anyone.

That gave me the confidence. *Alex likes me.* "To be honest, none of them were my type."

His blue eyes danced. "What is your type, Ky?"

"I like my men tall, dark, and handsome," I said with a grin as I got up and moved toward him.

"You do?" His eyes never left mine.

Nodding, I stepped even closer toward him. "I tend to like my men a bit older. They're more mature, you know what I mean?"

His Adam's apple bobbed in his throat as I sat next to him, so close our outer thighs touched. "You mean like ten or so years older?"

"Yeah." Turning to face him, I felt my robe open a little. He looked at my chest more than once. Alex is waking up the inner whore who has been sedated for a long, long time.

His fingers brushed my cheek. "I bet you looked beautiful."

"Some guy did call me sexy." Moving slowly, I reached out and ran my hands up his arms, then rested them on his broad shoulders. How I knew what to do is beyond me.

"You really slapped that guy?" he asked with a sexy grin. "You're not just telling me that?"

"You seem to be getting jealous, Alex." My eyes could not leave his lips as they inched closer to mine. "You might think I made that up to pacify you, but it's the truth. I slapped the asshole. And I would do it again to any guy who took my hand and pressed it against his erection."

"You would?" He stopped his progression, taking a moment of precaution.

Nodding, I let him know, "Yep, I would slap anyone who ever did that again. Save one man. Now that man, well, he could do anything he wants."

My chest heaved as I held my breath. Alex's eyes were on my lips, and I felt the heat rising inside of me. "Is that one man, me?" His eyes flew up to mine.

"Yeah," I whispered. "It's you, Alex."

He smiled, and then his lips moved in and fell on mine with an unimaginable softness. The way his hands reached up and held my face left me breathless. His tongue pushed through my lips, parting them so he could explore inside.

The fire that ripped through me frightened me at first. He moved his tongue in a playful fashion, running it over mine, and mine reciprocated.

The scary feeling subsided, and something else came over me. Lust. Passion. Desire. And then arose my need for him.

My insides pulsed to my heartbeat, juices began to flow in ways I had no idea could happen. My panties became wet as my body wanted more.

To feel him inside of me! I wanted to climb onto his lap and ride him for days at a time. And I wanted that to happen right then and there.

When he pushed me onto my back, I quickly spread my legs around him, and he moved his body between them. Something hard, long, and fat mashed against my throbbing pussy. I moved my hands down and felt the outline of his hard dick. A groan escaped me as I ran my hand up and down the length.

With one tug, he had my robe untied and pushed it away to uncover my body. His hand grabbed one of my tits. Pushing down the top of my nightgown, he exposed the breast, then played with the nipple until it was hard.

I gasped with the somewhat painful sensation, and he kissed me harder—so hard our teeth clashed. It took my mind off the pain and back to him. His body moved in waves against mine. Our sexes ground together.

I could smell it in the air, the sweet sexual scents that seeped out of us. It made me heady, and I felt drunk. I'd never been drunk! My first experience and I'd gotten drunk on Alex's kiss.

When his lips finally left mine, grazing them along my neck, I whimpered, "No, kiss me again."

His chest moved as he groaned, then his lips came back to mine. Another kiss took me to new heights. His hands moved all over me, touching everything he could reach and leaving trails of fire in their path.

Somehow, he managed to get my nightgown completely off the top half of my body, and when he pulled his mouth away again, he dove for one tit and sucked it as he played with the other.

I ran my hands through his hair, moaning as each suck he made had my belly going tight, and something incredible happened inside of me. "I can't believe it feels like this. No wonder people do this."

Maybe I'd been missing out? His tongue moved over the tip of my nipple over and over. I'd been missing out. But was I feeling all this because anyone could make me feel this way, or was it because it was Alex?

He moved one hand down between us; I felt the back of it brush my pussy as he tried to undo his pants. It was about to happen. I was about to lose my virginity. And I was so ready!

Pushing down his boxers, he took my hand then placed it on his cock. It's skin was surprisingly soft as I ran my hand up and down while he still sucked my tit.

"I had no idea," I whispered as I moved my hand up and down the long shaft.

Pulling his mouth off my tit, he looked at me. "What do you mean, you had no idea?"

"That it would feel this way."

He moved my hand off his cock looking uneasy. "Ky, how far have you gone with a man before?"

He had to know the truth. "You're my first kiss, Alex."

"Shit!" He pulled away from me! What was suddenly so wrong? "I knew it."

"You knew I was a virgin?" I sat up, pulling my robe back around to cover my body.

He nodded. "I'm sorry. I shouldn't have done this."

And then he was gone, leaving me alone and wondering what to do now.

11

ALEX

A WEEK WENT by with me saying very little to Ky. I made a terrible mistake and had to back things up. There was no way I could take that girl's virginity without being able to make a commitment to her.

Rachelle's sickness and eventual death hadn't soured me on women, but it allowed me to experience things that went along with being committed to another human being. With love comes pain—it was that simple. I had enough pain to last me a lifetime; I wasn't looking for more of the same.

Sitting at the desk in my home office, the hour was late, and I needed to go to bed. But I hadn't slept well since that night. Leaving Ky wasn't easy; it had taken a lot of willpower. But I couldn't hurt her if we'd gone any further.

I genuinely liked the girl. Even her social awkwardness was cute. And the way she interacted with my daughter did things to my heart I didn't know were possible.

Earlier that day, I sat on the back patio, watching Ky and Tabby running around the playground in the park behind the house. Ky didn't care how silly she behaved; she only cared Tabby was having fun and laughing.

Chewing my lower lip, I asked myself, "How long will you let this go on?"

How long could I possibly stay away from Ky? How long could I go without saying more than a few words to her? How long could I keep my hands and kisses off her, now that I'd tasted those sweet lips?

Innocent or not, that girl's kiss took me to a place I'd never been before. I had no idea if it was her or the amount of time that had passed without me having sexual contact with anyone, but touching her, feeling her? It had done me in.

If I slept with Ky—if I took her virginity—then I would fall in love with her. There was no doubt in my mind that it could consume us both. I found that out the hard way with Rachelle.

When you love someone, you experience the pain they do. When they die, they take a part of you with them. It leaves an emptiness nothing and no one can fill.

If I did fall in love with Ky, there would still be this hole where Rachelle had dug into me, taking a piece of my soul with her when she left our daughter and me behind. If I gave my heart to Ky and took hers, it would put me back in danger of losing another piece of myself. And I couldn't take that and function well enough to take care of my daughter.

With nothing settling in my brain, I decided to go to bed anyway. Sure, I'd toss and turn, but at least my body would be in a state of relaxation, I hoped.

When I got to the staircase, she was sitting there on the top step waiting for me.

"Alex, I can't take this anymore." Ky's eyes were dark and drooped in a way that made my heart ache.

I did this to her.

Not taking one step, I said, "I should've kept my hands to myself, Ky. I'm sorry."

"I'm not," she said with a sigh punctuating her sentence. "You're scared."

I didn't like anyone to think I was afraid of anything. "Am not."

"Yes, you are." She ran her hands down her legs that were covered with the white robe she wore.

The last thing I should've been thinking about was what she wore underneath that robe, but I couldn't help myself. I shook my head to clear the thoughts that popped up. "Look, I'm not afraid. I just don't know what to do after the fact—do you get what I'm saying?"

Her eyes bore into me. "Do you honestly think you will just *hit it then quit it*, Alex?"

I couldn't help but laugh at the way she put it. "I might do that to you. It wouldn't have anything to do with you or what we'd done. *I'd* be the problem. And it's not that I'm scared—but I've been through a lot, and I'm not sure having a relationship is worth the pain that can come along with it."

"I understand." She stood, then held out her hands. "Come on, Alex. I'll take my chances."

Easy for her to say, she had no idea what it honestly felt like to lose a piece of yourself when the other half of you is ripped away. But the way she looked as she waited at the top of those stairs took my breath away.

Her silky hair fell in loose waves around her shoulders. Her skin glowed under the dim light. And her curves couldn't be hidden by that robe. The robe covered what? "Are you naked underneath?"

"There's only one way to find out," she coaxed. "Come on up, Alex. I've done nothing but fantasize about you and me since that night. I can't take it any longer. I've never wanted anyone in my life. Now that I've found this need for you, it won't stop. I can't sleep, eat, or even think—except about how it would be with you. If you give me nothing else, give me the gift of having you as my first. Alex, I've never even had an orgasm."

My cock went hard, and my heart sped up. I never had a virgin before, and to find out that she never even experienced an orgasm? What else could I do? The way my body reacted to her words... My mind wasn't getting in the way.

Ky was going through the same things by not giving in to what we both wanted so badly. I took the stairs two at a time. "Promise me you won't be hurt if I can't give you more, okay?" I still had to guard my heart after all.

She nodded. "Kiss me, Alex. Take me to my bed and make me into a woman."

"Shit!" My cock strained against my jeans, and it proved most painful. Scooping her up, I carried her down the hall.

Hurrying to her room, I barely got the door closed behind us before she ran her hands through my hair, then locked her lips on mine. Her breath sweet, her tongue demanding, she took my breath away with that kiss.

Putting her feet on the floor, I tugged the belt of that robe, letting it fall open to reveal she was indeed naked underneath. It seemed she was prepared to do anything to get me to take her.

Ky wasn't the girl I thought her to be. When she wanted something, she'd use everything she had to get it. And I found that super fucking hot. "Damn, girl. You came prepared, didn't you?"

"I couldn't take another night of torture, Alex." Her hands moved under my sweater and then she pulled it over my head. Her eyes were shining as she ran her hands over my chest, lingering over the anchor tat on my left pec. She kissed it, then whispered, "I haven't thanked you for your years of service to our country, Alex. Let me show you how thankful I really am."

She sank to her knees in front of me, and I nearly gasped as she undid my jeans, pulling them down, then she did the same thing to my blue boxers. Her eyes went wide as she saw my cock, erect just for her; it made me smile. "Is this the first dick you've ever seen, Ky?"

"It is." She licked her lips. "I've watched a few videos about blow jobs. I practiced on a cucumber. Can I give it a try?"

"Hell yes!" I leaned back on the door as she rubbed her hands together to warm them.

"If I hurt you just let me know, 'Kay?" she asked as she looked up at me with the most innocent eyes I'd ever seen before getting sucked off.

"I doubt you'll hurt me, but I promise to let you know." I grinned. "Can I come in your mouth?"

Looking apprehensive, she said, "Better stop me before that. I don't want to throw up and ruin things."

Nodding, I'd thought as much. "Awritey, then."

Softly, she stroked my cock, then put her lips on the tip, making me see stars already. Her mouth moved over it, surrounding it with more heat than it had seen in a very long time. Ky moaned as she took it all in and I sighed.

Moving slowly, I watched her head going back and forth and nearly lost it several times as she gently sucked me. Just as I was about to blow, I stopped her, "Ky, that's all I can take."

The smile she wore when she pulled her mouth off me was sultry and sexy. "Now you'll take my virginity?"

She lay back on the floor, the robe spread out behind her. I wasn't about to take her for the first time on a hard floor. Picking her up, I carried her to the bed where I laid her down and took the robe away.

Looking at her naked body, running my fingers lightly over every inch of it, I sighed. I couldn't make love to this gorgeous woman only one time. But could I give myself to her, heart and soul? "Ky, are you sure about this? There's no going back once we do this. I might never be able to give you anything more than sex. Please understand that. It's not personal. I like you a lot and think you're great. But I don't have much of a heart to give to anyone."

Her eyes glazed over as she looked at me. "Alex, I'll be okay with whatever happens. I promise you. Now please fill this void I've had until you kissed me that night."

"Well, since I caused it..." I couldn't have stopped myself at that moment. Moving my body over hers, I spread her legs, then pressed the tip of my cock against her virgin hole. "You ready?" Quick to penetrate would be the best way to begin.

Her nails cut into the flesh of my shoulders as she nodded. "Do it."

I kissed her, softly at first, then passion overtook me as my cock throbbed and the blood rushed into it at the pressure it felt at the cusp of that virgin pussy. With one hard thrust, I broke through her hymen.

Ky's scream was smothered by my kiss; tears fell down her cheeks with my hard and fast thrusts. The hot blood of her broken purity was mixing with her natural juices.

I'd taken it away from her—her innocence. *Now to see if I can give her something in return.*

12

KY

With every movement he made, the pain was less and less. At first, I'd thought it was a mistake in begging Alex to take my virginity. His cock was massive—certainly not what a virgin should take on for her first go at it. But my desire wasn't fading, so I went with it. What was painful at first turned into something I couldn't have ever guessed would feel the way it did.

Panting, I commented, "Alex, it feels like something's welling up inside of me."

"You're about to orgasm," he let me know. "Close your eyes and let it happen."

Closing my eyes, I felt the sensation growing as if a wave was forming. And then it all came crashing down. "Ah! Oh, God! Alex!" Pure pleasure filled every cell of my body. I swore even my hair felt the electricity. My toes curled, and I arched up to meet his hard thrusts.

I want more.

His mouth closed down on mine as he went even faster and harder. His pelvis rubbed against my clit, and it was swelling, then his mouth left mine as he made a savage groan, "Fuck!"

Wet heat filled me, and my body reacted by having another orgasm just as his cock jerked inside of me. "Oh, hell!" I dug my fingernails into his back, and then up until I felt his hair. My fingers pulled his hair as our bodies were racked with ecstasy.

He went still on top of me, his head resting on my breasts. Both of us panted like animals, then I kissed the top of his head. "Thank you, Alex," I breathed.

His hands moved along my waist then up my sides as his hot breath ran over my tits. "Thank you, Ky."

Playing with his dark hair, I felt at ease with him. "That was mind-blowing."

"I'm glad you thought so." He raised his head to look at me, not bothering to pull his dick out of me. "You're my first virgin."

I bit my tongue so I wouldn't say *his last virgin.* Already, I didn't want to share this man. "Glad I could be the first for you, too, then."

He kissed me softly and rolled off me, leaving me with a cold feeling. "I'll let you get some sleep."

Rolling on my side, I felt the gush of wetness as it flowed out of me. "Yeah, I'll be able to sleep now."

I'll have to shower first, but then I'll sleep like a baby.

He stood there for a moment, gloriously naked. "Ky, that was spectacular."

"Was it?" I had no idea if that was ordinary or amazing. It felt the latter, but I had nothing to compare it to.

"Yeah." He reached out, running his hand along my jaw line. "I've got a lot to think about. 'Night."

I didn't know what that meant, nor did I care. My body still pulsed from the orgasms, and my mind was still drunk on what we'd done.

After he left my room, I went to take a shower, finding a ghastly mess from losing my virginity. "Yuck." I hoped it wouldn't be that messy every time.

Alex was honest with me. There might not be more. But then again, he said it might just be sex. Just having sex would be fine with me.

That man could sneak into my bed anytime, and I'd welcome him with open arms and legs.

After showering, I went back to bed, finding it a mess as well. As I removed the sheets off the bed, I thought about the maid cleaning them, and I couldn't have that. The staff shouldn't know what we'd done. No one should.

What would people think of Alex if they knew he screwed the *au pair*?

A prestigious doctor, thirteen years older than me and with a young daughter, Alex would be ridiculed if they knew what we'd done.

Gathering the linens, I put my robe back on, then took the stained white sheets down to the laundry to do them myself. Putting the washing machine on cold, I first rinsed the blood off sheets, and then added plenty of bleach. Spotting some stain remover, I sprayed it on the remainder of the stains before shoving them into the washer.

As the red was disappearing, I felt somewhat melancholy. How quickly the pleasure and warmth faded away sort of frightened me. But things had to go on; one couldn't live in that state of euphoria for long.

Taking another set of white sheets from the linen closet, I went back to put them on the bed. Walking into the room, I could still smell Alex in there. His unique scent lingered, and I hoped it would stay that way.

Then I thought about the maid coming in the morning to clean and lit a scented wax warmer to get rid of the scent that brought me so much peace.

We'll have to hide this now. How do I feel about that? My first bond and I had to hide it.

What Alex and I had was not a relationship. He'll probably want to fuck some more. I hoped he did anyway.

If the time before our tryst left me with sleepless nights, no appetite, and no clear thinking, any refusal by him to have sex with me again would be worse.

I made that damn promise to him.

Climbing into the bed after making it, I could still feel the warmth where we laid. Smiling, I moved to the side of that warm spot and ran my hand over it.

"This was the place where Alex and I became one. Even if it was for a short time, we had become one." I closed my eyes, reliving that moment.

So harsh at first, then utterly mind-blowing; it was the best thing I'd ever done. There would never be regrets as to who I had my first sexual experience with. No matter what, Alex was the right man to have taken my virginity.

Thinking about my future and what that would hold had me feeling a little sad. *What if Alex and I don't have a future together?*

Could I ever let another man do to me what I let Alex do?

I didn't want to think about that. I didn't want to think about Alex and me either. It was useless to think he and I could ever be anything real.

With no idea what tomorrow would bring, I fell asleep, sleeping soundly for the first time since I'd met the man.

Waking up the next morning to Tabby's voice on the baby monitor, "I'm up, Ky," I rolled out of bed, finding myself stiff and hardly able to walk.

"Shit," I whispered. Then I hit the button on the monitor. "Okay, Tabby. I'll be right there, Honey."

Putting on a nightgown and then a robe, I slipped my feet into slippers and went out the door only to find Alex there, dressed and smiling at me.

"Morning, Ky."

Now I felt awkward as hell. "Um- hi."

I didn't know what we should do, but saying hi wasn't it. A good morning kiss seemed to be the normal. But we weren't a typical couple.

"I'll take care of Tabby this morning." He gestured to the way I held my legs apart unnaturally. "You should go soak in a hot tub for a while. That should help with the soreness. And here, take some ibuprofen. You've got the morning off. I'll make my rounds later today."

"Okay." I still didn't know how to act. "Thanks."

I turned to go back into my suite when he said quietly, "I really had a great time last night."

"Me, too." A blush heated my cheeks, and I retreated into the room before he saw that. Leaning on the door, I tried to catch my breath. "Oh, hell. How am I going to do this?"

After a long, hot bath, I wore a dress because the way the jeans felt against my crotch was awful. How long will it take for the ibuprofen to kick in? Should I expect to feel this way every time we had sex?

When I went down to take over for Alex with Tabby, I found them in her playroom. His broad smile greeted me as Tabby ran to me. I picked her up, giggling as she kissed my cheek. "Finally!"

"Did you miss me, Tabby?" I asked her as I put her back down.

"Yeah! Bunches." She twirled around, letting her dress spin around. "Daddy put this one on me, and I wanted to show you, but he wouldn't let me go into your room. Are you sick?"

I shook my head. "No. Your daddy gave me the morning off, so I slept in. But your dress is very pretty."

Tabby ran her hand over the soft fabric of my dress. "Yours is pretty, too. Let's go to lunch and show our pretty dresses today."

Alex got up off the sofa and pulled out his wallet, taking out his credit card. "Here you go, Ky. Take her out, and then maybe visit a museum or something? You both look way too beautiful to stay cooped up at home today." He winked at me as he handed me the card, grazing his fingers along my palm.

My breath hitched in my throat and the way moisture pooled between my legs told me that man could take me right there and I'd let him do it. "OK. we'll go out today."

"I have to work." He walked away and I felt this tremendous urge to kiss him. "I'll be home for dinner. After that, you and I need to have a meeting, Ky."

"About?" I asked.

He turned to look at me as he opened the door. "Things." He

wore absolutely no expression. What kinds of things did he want to talk to me about? Why did he call it *a meeting*?

"Should I be worried?" I asked him frowning.

"You should not be, Ky." He cocked his head to one side. "After what we talked about before, I thought you understood things."

Last night I would've said anything to get him to fuck me. Now though, what I would do if he didn't want to have sex anymore? I nodded and tried to play it cool. "OK. See you at dinner then, Alex. Have a nice day at work."

"You, too." And then he was gone.

And I have no idea where we stand.

13

ALEX

Whistling as I walked down the hall toward the emergency room to see a patient who'd come in after falling and hitting her head, I couldn't help the great mood I was in.

As crazy as it might've seemed, letting her in wasn't going to hurt me. Something told me not to worry and just live, laugh, and love. Yes—something inside told me it was okay to love Ky.

Who knew sex would make me feel whole again? But it wasn't just the sex—it was Ky. Ky was the only one who'd ever gotten to me that way. Even Rachelle hadn't affected me the way Ky did.

And Rachelle had quite the effect on me. I'd fallen in love with her at first sight. I knew Rachelle was the one right from the start. What I didn't realize was there could be more than just one woman who could be the one for me.

Not that I was ready to propose, but only to be in a relationship with Ky. I was so prepared, it didn't seem real.

Nurse Jamison stood in front of a curtain. Her hands on her hips, she gave me a look that said we were dealing with a mentally unstable person. "Glad you're here, Dr. Arlen. Mrs. Higginson is worried and needs your help right away."

"Okay." I pulled the curtain back to find a woman in her seventies with—of all things—a feminine napkin taped to her forehead. "Did you bandage that yourself, ma'am?"

"I did," she said as she crossed her arms in front of her chest. "And that nurse of yours wanted to take it off. I told her blood would come gushing out, and I didn't want the bandage removed until a doctor was around to stitch me up."

Pulling on some gloves, I approached her to make the removal and found her holding up her hands to stop me.

"Don't you want me to fix you up?"

Her pale blue eyes glistened with unshed tears. "It really hurts."

I saw no evidence of blood on the backside of the pad and had no idea what kind of wound she had. "I'll be very careful. I promise."

Batting her eyelashes, she nodded. "Okay then. I trust you."

Easing the thing off her delicate skin, I removed the pad to find nothing, not even a bump. "When did this happen, Mrs. Higginson?"

"About an hour ago. I fell out of my bed and onto the floor. I hit my head on the nightstand. There was blood everywhere." The way she looked at me told me she really thought that happened.

Turning to the nurse, I let her know she needed to get the paperwork ready to admit the woman. "Get her admitted for the night, Nurse Jamison." I turned my attention to the patient once again. "Did you drive yourself here or did someone bring you?"

"I don't have anyone to count on, Doc. I drove myself." She reached up to feel the spot on her head she thought was injured. Then her reality appeared to dawn on her. "Oh no. What's happened? I swear there was a gash on my forehead. I swear it!"

"Not to worry," I tried to calm her. "I'm sure we can get to the bottom of this. We'll run some tests right away. Do you have someone I could call to let them know you'll be here?"

"My neighbor. My cat will need to be fed." She looked even more distraught. "But I can't recall her phone number. And I can't recall if I locked my front door when I left. And I might've let the cat out, too." She began to wring her hands in her lap. "I've got to get back home, Doc. I can't stay. I just can't."

"I tell you what, give me your address, and I'll have someone go by your home and make sure things are locked up for you, and your cat is put back inside if it got out." I took out my cell to call Ky, the only person I could think of on short notice who'd do what the woman needed. "My girlfriend won't mind helping you out. I'll have her go to the neighbor's house, too, to let them know."

"You'd do all that for me?" she asked with wide eyes that looked like they were about to tear up. Her hand shook as she reached out to touch my hand as I made the call to Ky. "Thank you, Doc. You're a real angel."

"You're welcome, Mrs. Higginson. And it's no trouble at all."

Ky answered my call, "Yes, Alex?"

"Hi." The sound of her voice gave me butterflies, and it was the most pleasant feeling in the world. "I've got a favor to ask of you."

"Okay."

"A patient here is a bit confused, and we're keeping her here for the night," I said.

Ky interrupted me, "So you won't be home when you said you would?"

"No, I'll be home when I said I would." The disappointment in her voice made me smile. "I'll be there for dinner, then we'll have our talk." I had so much to tell her about my breakthrough and how it was all because of her. "I need you to go to this lady's home and make sure things are secure. She's got a cat she's worried about. It belongs in the house, and it might be outside. And her neighbor needs know where she is. Ask her if she'll make sure the cat's fed while Mrs. Higginson is here."

"Okay," Ky said. "Text me the address, and Steven can take us over there. Tabby, we've got to go, Honey. Daddy has an errand for us."

"'Kay, Ky," I heard Tabby say.

My heart felt so full—and over something so small, too. It was amazing, the transformation one night with Ky had made. "Thanks,

Ky. I really appreciate that. I hate to interrupt your little outing. But it's for a good cause."

"I know it is. We don't mind at all, do we, Tabby?" Ky asked.

"Not at all," Tabby said.

Ky was an excellent influence on my daughter. I'd chosen the right nanny for her. And I was sure I picked the right woman for me, too. "Thanks. I'll see you at home for dinner. Bye."

The way the woman looked at me had me feeling weird. "She says she's happy for you, Alex."

"Who?" I looked behind me at where her eyes now focused. I didn't see anyone there.

"Her," she said as she pointed to the spot just behind me. "The pretty lady with the long blonde hair. "She says it's time and that she loves you and loves how well you're taking care of Tabby." Mrs. Higginson blinked a few times, then her eyes came back to mine. "I'm sorry. What were you saying?"

"I wasn't saying anything," I told her. "You were. Did you see someone standing behind me?"

She looked upset, then put her hands on her stomach. "My tummy hurts. Why does my tummy hurt?" Looking back at the place behind me, she shouted, "Go away! You're hurting me!"

What was going on? The woman might have seen Rachelle. Her stomach hurt her a lot at the very end of her life. I turned to the spot she must've been. Unfortunately, I saw nothing. "Rachelle?"

"She's gone." Mrs. Higginson sighed with relief. "Sometimes that happens. When someone died in a lot of pain, I can feel it, too. It's a curse that comes along with the gift of being able to see spirits. She left when I told her she hurt me. They most often do leave when I let them know that."

Shocked, I nodded as if that made perfect sense, which it did not. But I felt better about my relationship with Ky knowing Rachelle was happy about it, too.

"How long have you been able to see spirits?" I asked her.

"Since I was a kid." She looked at me with confusion. "Maybe it was someone else who hit their head, Doc. Maybe I was asleep when one of them came to me, and I got befuddled. I can go home now. I'm okay."

She was not okay. "Since you came here for help, we're going to help you. You might be right, you might be fine, but we have equipment to make sure of that."

"You think I'm crazy, don't you?" She was used to people telling her that.

"I don't." I wasn't sure of my thoughts about the woman. "I wouldn't be doing right by you if you leave without doing these tests. So please allow me to run them, and when we find you're fine, you can leave. Deal?" I hoped she'd make the deal. I knew how stubborn some people could be. So when she nodded, it made me smile. "Good. Thank you."

A few hours later, with the tests done, I found that Mrs. Higginson had experienced a small stroke. But she'd be fine with time. It was early enough so the medication we gave her would work on her brain.

Going home, I was happy with how the day had gone. There were things I wanted to talk to Ky about she'd find agreeable, too.

At dinner, Ky was quiet and even a bit shy. It must've been because she had no idea how I felt about what we'd done. But she'd soon find out after Tabby went to bed.

Just before leaving the table, I looked Ky in the eyes. "I'll be in my office. After you get Tabby to sleep, we'll have our meeting there."

She looked kind of sick as she nodded. I couldn't say anything else in front of Tabby or the kitchen staff who'd come in to clean up. But later, when Ky came into my office, I got up out of my chair and met her halfway, taking her in my arms and kissing her the way I wanted to all day.

Her body melted in my arms and when the kiss ended, she looked at me with shining eyes. "So, does this mean we keep doing what we've started?"

"I don't want to end this!" I kissed her again then managed to pull myself back. "This Friday, Tabby's grandparents are picking her up to take her to visit some of their relatives in New York. It'll be a four-day weekend for us."

"Us?" she asked with a sexy smile on her luscious lips.

"Yes, us." I couldn't help it and kissed her again before going on, "I've booked us three nights in a private resort in the Florida Keys. It'll be our first real date."

Burying her head in my chest, she hugged me tightly. "That sounds unbelievably good, Alex." Then she raised her head to look at me. "You've made me very happy. I've been worried all day that you'd want to stop this. And I didn't want to stop."

Neither did I.

14

KY

WHILE STILL FEELING as if I was living in a dream world, one thing wasn't dreamlike at all: the fact we still had to keep our relationship secret from everyone. The staff couldn't get a whiff of our doings after Tabby went to sleep. That meant I had to wash my sheets each night.

As I stood there in the laundry room the morning Tabby would leave with her grandparents, I got a chill when I thought about going away with Alex the next day and getting to be a couple in front of everyone for a change.

Walking hand in hand down the beach wouldn't be a thing we could do while in Seattle. We always kept our distance from each other in front of others. It had to be that way. Not knowing where things were heading with us, it made more sense to keep everyone else out of our private affairs.

Pulling the clean sheets out of the dryer, I folded them and put them in the place of the ones I'd already taken to make the bed back up. Getting up in time to beat the maids from finding the linens in the dryer wasn't easy, but I managed to get it done each morning.

Going back to my room, I found Alex coming out of his. "It's only five a.m., what are you doing up?"

Alex looked at me like a deer in the headlights. "What are you doing up so early, Ky?"

"The sheets," I crossed my arms over my chest, noticing he was dressed and ready to leave. "Did you get a call from the hospital?"

"No." His lips formed one thin line and he looked flustered. "I have to meet someone before work. And Tabby's grandparents will be here around noon today. I want to finish my rounds before they get here."

All I heard was he had to meet someone. "And who is this person you're meeting at the crack of dawn, Alex?"

"Someone who has something I want." He looked even more flustered as he kicked the carpet with the toe of his shoe. "Look, it's a surprise alright? For this weekend. And I need to get it this morning since we're leaving later today."

"Whoa, I thought we're not leaving until tomorrow." He'd upped the trip on me unexpectedly. "I'm not even packed."

"Yeah, about that. You don't have to pack." He frowned. "Damn, baby. You're making the surprise difficult! Don't worry about packing a thing; it's all taken care of."

"Are you buying me some clothes, Alex?" I smiled, thinking how thoughtful. He must've known I didn't own any beach clothes. "I planned to buy some things once we got to Florida."

"Well, you won't have to worry about that." Moving closer to me, he ran his arms around me, then kissed the tip of my nose.

"You hate my taste in clothes, don't you?" He didn't need to answer. He probably hated the way I dressed. The fact was I hadn't bought many new clothes.

"I do not." He bit his lower lip. "But you need nicer outfits, and I don't want to waste time shopping. That's all. You're as cute as a button, Ky. You know that. I'm saving us time so we can do better things than shop while we've got this free time."

"When you put it that way, it makes sense. So who is selling these clothes?"

"Reagan." He looked pleased with himself. "You mentioned she was pretty that day you met her. And she has a great sense of style. So I asked her if she'd mind shopping for you."

"That means you've told her about us."

"She guessed it." He smiled, then kissed me again. "She said I looked like a new man, and there had to be a reason for that. Then she put two and two together along with the jealous way you acted, and she deduced that you were the special lady in my life."

"I hope you swore her to secrecy, Alex." It wouldn't be good for this to get out.

Shrugging, he said, "I don't care what anyone thinks, Ky."

What is he talking about? "Why do you think I've been washing the sheets every night? It's so the staff won't find out about us."

"No one asked you to do that," he reminded me.

"Well, you can't be slamming the baby sitter, Alex." My eyes rolled as for once *I* wasn't the most naïve person in the world.

Kissing my cheek, he led me to my bedroom door. "I've got things to do, Ky. Get back in bed. And stop worrying about the stupid sheets."

Doing as he said, I got back into the bed, then snuggled down, wondering what he meant.

Is he ready to come out with our relationship? Surely not.

After waking back up, I got Tabby ready for her grandparents, packing up her things for the four-night and five-day trip. She was all smiles as she helped. "And my unicorn nightgown."

"It's in your middle drawer in the closet. Can you go get it for me?" I asked.

"Yes!" She ran to get it, then came back with it in her little hand. "Here. My nightlight, too?"

I held up the princess nightlight. "It's right here."

"Good." She took my hand after I zipped the suitcase. "I will miss you."

Picking her up, I hugged her. "I'll miss you, too. But don't worry; when you get back we'll do all kinds of things again. And you can tell me all about how much fun you had on your trip. I want you to have a very good time with them. And give them lots of hugs and kisses, too, okay?"

"Yes! Hugs and kisses!" she exclaimed.

Carrying her downstairs, I held her bag in my free hand and felt sad knowing it would be five days before I could see her sweet little face again. *But her father will keep me entertained*, I thought wickedly.

As I got to the foyer to leave her suitcase there, Mr. Randolph came out of nowhere to open the door. "The Vanderhavens are here."

Nerves shot through me. It was the first time I'd ever be meeting them, and there I was having a secret affair with their late daughter's husband. "Oh, Alex wanted to be here when they arrived."

I needed him as a buffer. What might come out of my mouth if he wasn't around to do that talking? But he wasn't there.

When the butler opened the door, I saw an older woman who resembled Tabby and a man with dove-white hair. Both were clad impeccably, she wearing a dress that probably cost a fortune, and he in a suit that looked expensive as well.

I put Tabby down so she could greet her grandparents and she ran to them. Her grandfather scooped her up as her grandmother ran her hand through her silky curls. I curled her hair, so she looked extra adorable.

"My, my, look at all these pretty curls. You look so sweet, Tabitha."

"Thank you, Grandmommy." Tabby kissed her grandmother's cheek, then took her grandfather's face between her little hands and kissed him, too. "I missed you, Grandfather."

She talked to them a bit formally, but everything about them seemed proper—all the way to the immaculate Bentley parked at the end of the walkway.

Standing there quietly, I didn't know what to say. But Mrs. Vanderhaven did. "You're the governess, aren't you?"

"I am." I extended my hand. "My name is Ky."

She shook it briefly. "And that is short for what, dear?"

"Kyla. My name's Kyla Rush, Mrs. Vanderhaven. It's nice to meet you." I looked at her husband. "And you, too, Mr. Vanderhaven."

Mr. Randolph urged us to move to another room, "This way please."

Everyone followed him to the small living area just off the foyer. I felt inadequate around them. They were so polished! "I packed a suitcase for Tabby."

"Good," her grandmother said. "We'd like to get on our way." Pulling a cell phone out of her Gucci purse, she made a call. "Alexander, where are you?"

She looked at her husband with disdain and whispered, "He's probably stuck at work."

He whispered, "He's a doctor, dear. These things happen. No reason to get upset."

"We can't wait, Alexander. Tell your daughter goodbye so we can get back to the airport." She handed the phone to Tabby.

"Daddy, we are going. I will miss you." She kissed the phone screen. "Bye, bye." Then she handed it back to her grandmother. "Here, Grandmommy."

I felt like crying and went to pick her up. "I'll carry her out for you."

"She can walk," her grandmother said. "She's not a baby." She eyed me and I put Tabby down. "You're much younger than I anticipated. Alexander didn't tell me your age. What are you, twenty or so?"

"I'm twenty-two." I put my hands behind my back, unsure of what to do with them. "I have a bachelor's degree in Early Childhood Development."

"And what kind of experience do you have?" she asked.

Her husband took her by the elbow. "Come now, Rebecca. Alexander has already hired the girl. You can't interview her now."

"Things aren't set in stone, Claus," she replied, making me flinch. "While *we* have our granddaughter, we *will* be watching for anything out of the ordinary with her. If we think she needs another babysitter, we will not hesitate to tell our son-in-law."

"I understand," I said quietly. "If it means anything to you, I adore and love Tabby. And I'm doing the best I can with her."

"I love Ky, too," Tabby said.

Even though I won Tabby over, I hadn't earned her grandmother's approval.

God, I hope they don't see anything detrimental in her.

15

ALEX

By the end of the day, Ky and I found ourselves lying on a deserted Florida beach, our private bungalow behind us and barely a thing on either of us.

"I knew Reagan would pick out an awesome bikini for you, Ky." I turned to my side, then lifted my head to look down at her gorgeous curvy body, running my fingers over her stomach and loving the way goose bumps covered her creamy flesh.

"It's a lot skimpier than anything I would've dared to buy myself," she said as she put her hand over mine to stop me from moving it. "That tickles."

Moving in to nibble her ear, I whispered, "It's supposed to." I bit her neck playfully, making her squeal.

I couldn't remember a time when I felt so full of life. The sex was off the chain. I'd never had better or more sex in my entire life. Ky fit me like a glove. I didn't know if that was because I was her first, but I loved the way it felt being inside of her.

The past week we spent every night going at it like wild rabbits. It cemented things for me. I knew it now—without a doubt—I've fallen in love with her. I couldn't see me ever wanting anyone else now that I'd had the very best.

And it was time Ky knew that. The insecurity was written all over her face at times. And the fact she thought to hide our relationship from everyone told me one of two things. Either she thought I wouldn't ever want to be with her out in the open or she didn't feel she was good enough for me. Either way, she was wrong.

Now she would know how I really felt about her. Looking into her eyes that the glowing sunlight had turned to a shade of green that nearly matched the ocean waves that tickled our feet, I wanted to let her know what she meant to me, "Kyla Rush." I thought about it for a moment then asked, "What's your middle name?"

"What's yours?" she asked with a sexy grin.

"Montgomery." I kissed her soft lips. "Now tell me yours."

Wrinkling her nose, she said, "I don't like it. I've never used it. Not really. It's so, *so* old sounding."

"Tell me, baby." I kissed her again. "It won't make me like you any less."

"It might," she said as she traced the tat on my chest. "And I'd hate it if you stopped liking me. I got used to you."

"I got used to you, too." I couldn't seem to keep my lips off hers. But I wanted to know her middle name. It was important for future reasons. "Okay, if you want any more kisses, you'll have to tell me what it is."

Her chest rose as she sighed so deeply it defied imagination. "Gertrude."

Kyla Gertrude Rush?

"It's not so bad." I almost laughed. "Gertie." It was cute when I thought about it. "Kyla Gertie."

Her brows furrowed. "Don't."

I got off track with her aversion to telling me her middle name. "Okay, I won't." My lips grazed hers. "I've got something to say, Ky. Something I've never told anyone, but the one woman I married and my daughter. And now I want to say it to you, and have you know I mean it. I'm not one to throw this phrase around lightly as some people do."

She put her hand on my chest, gazing at me as the sun began to set over the water, covering her skin with a bronze glow. The highlights in her hair shone even more, and I couldn't remember a time when she'd been more beautiful. "Tell me, Alex."

Her chest stopped moving. She was holding her breath, so I wasted no time, "I love you, Kyla Gertrude Rush."

She closed her eyes, then smiled. "Wow. Even using that atrocious name, that still sounds good." When she opened them back up, I saw tears shimmering in them. "I love you, too, Alexander Montgomery Arlen."

With that out there, I hoped she'd never think I wanted to hide us again. "From now on, I never want you to feel you've got to hide anything about us. I'm going to move you into my bedroom when we get back."

Her expression turned worried. "What about Tabby? What's she going to think about that? I'm her nanny, Alex."

"She's three; she doesn't think in terms of you being hired to care for her. All she knows is that you love her and take care of her. She'll be happy about us. I'm sure she will." I kissed her again, and this time I took it further, wanting to *show* her how much I loved her, too.

Pulling her on top of me, I liked the weight of her. It had felt like a dream the last week. Some of that probably came from hiding we were crazy for each other. Those days were over now.

Pulling her lips off mine, Ky sat up, pulling my hands up to cup her 38 Ds. "Alex, as much as I want this, I don't want you ridiculed at work or home."

Why would she think anyone would taunt me if I had a hot young woman at my side? "baby, what the hell are you talking about? Who in their right mind would mock me for being with you?"

She moved my hands off her tits as a frown curved her lips. "The people you work with. That one lady won't, but others might. I'm thirteen years younger—and your baby sitter, too. It's kind of poor quality, don't you think?"

"No. People don't care about stuff like that. And who cares if they do? The only thing that matters to me is if you care. Which I hope you don't." It occurred to me all of a sudden that Ky might be embarrassed by my age. "Hey, you can be honest with me. I want you to know that. Are you not cool with being seen with me?"

"God, no!" She laughed and looked up at the darkening sky. "You're hot—like smoking hot. And you're a doctor, too. You're way out of my league. I'm fortunate you give me the time of day."

She had no idea the power she had. "Ky, you're gorgeous, baby. Any man would be lucky to have you. I mean that. You have no idea about the men that look your way, do you?"

She laughed as if she thought I was kidding. "Come on; no one looks at me, Alex. You're trying to boost my self-esteem."

"Am not." I couldn't believe her. "You know what? I'm taking you out to a Miami nightclub tonight to show you how attractive to the opposite sex you truly are. But you're mine, right? No one gets to touch what's mine."

"*Vice versa*," she said as she narrowed her eyes. "I don't want to share you. With the *I love yous* out of the way, it seems that time has arrived."

The idea that Ky wanted me to herself got me all tingly. "You do things to me no one ever has, Ky Rush."

"That's saying something, isn't it?" She moved her body back down, then our lips met, and she took me away with her kiss. A kiss, no longer sweet and innocent, but now sensual and sure.

Ky had matured so much in a week's time; it amazed me. The shy girl all but gone, she was ravenous in bed and expressed what she desired and what she wanted to do to me. It was unbelievable that a bashful girl like that could become so damn great in the sack.

And only I would ever get to have her. I wasn't about to let that girl go. I knew someday in the future I would change her last name.

When I had a diamond in my hands, I didn't drop it the way some men did. My head didn't turn to look at other women when I fell in love. Ky had a secure future with me, even if she didn't realize that yet.

Straddling me, Ky moved her body in a way that the thin material of our bathing suits didn't obstruct. Her tits brushed against my bare chest until the top rubbed off them. Her hard nipples rubbing against my skin, I moved her to put my mouth around one.

Her moans made my heart pound and my cock throb. But when I went to push my swimming trunks down, she stopped me. "We need to get ready to go out, remember? No sex until after. It'll be ten times hotter if we wait." She pulled herself up, then I saw pure joy on her face. "Oh! We could try doing it in the bathroom at the club. How funky would that be?"

I loved that about her. "I think it wouldn't be the funkiest thing I've ever heard of, but def for us."

Climbing off me, she held out her hand to help me up. "Come on. Let's take a shower, but no sex, OK? It'll be hotter if we're starving for each other when we get into that bathroom."

"So what you're saying is we're going to tease each other until somewhere around the end of the night, and then you'll give it to me?" I liked the way she thought. "Sounds enticing."

Taking me by the hand, she led me into the bungalow. "Not sure about that, but it'll be off the charts. Now that I know how fun sex is, I can't stop thinking about all the different ways we can do it." She stopped and looked at me with a serious expression. "Alex, have I become a nymphomaniac?"

"No." I didn't want Ky to change a single thing. "You love me. And I love you. And we're just expressing it in a physical way. What's wrong with that?"

"Hopefully, nothing. It's new to me, that's all." She started walking again. "My friend, Carla, says sex is mandatory. I can see why she's always said that now. But it's too intimate to do with just anyone. I'll never trust anyone the way I trust you, Alex."

And it better stay that way.

16

KY

I KEPT PULLING down at the bottom of the insanely short dress from the suitcase full of clothing his colleague bought for me. "Red isn't my color, Alex." I tugged the plunging neckline up, making the dress move up my thighs once more. "And I can't seem to get this skimpy thing to cover my tits and my ass at the same time."

"Red *is* your color, baby." He slipped his arms around me from behind as we danced to a Latin beat in the largest nightclub we could find. "And I like all the skin you're showing tonight. But I'll cover your ass if you feel too exposed." His lips pressed against my neck, flooding me instantly with desire.

Running my hand along his side, I stopped when I got to his hair, then tugged it as his kiss drove me wild. We moved in waves as the music continued. I danced so well with Alex! Somehow, with him, my body moved in impossible ways.

The club was packed, and the heat was close to unbearable. A cool ocean breeze just outside the club began calling my name. "Do you want to go outside for some fresh air, Alex?"

"Sure." He moved his hands down my body until he had one of my hands, then led me out of the cluster of gyrating people.

As we stepped outside, the cool air moved over the abundance of skin I had showing and felt better right away. "It's so hot in there." I fanned myself to cool down quicker.

His eyes raked over me. "It was just the sight of you that had me feeling so hot."

I smacked him on the shoulder. "You'll give me a big head if you don't stop with all the flattery." I pulled at the bottom of my dress again, but he stopped me.

"It's supposed to fit that way, Ky." Walking backward, he took me with him, sneaking around the side of the building. "Come with me, my little harlot."

Never in my wildest dreams did I think I'd ever be so free and easy sexually. Alex made it simple. I followed without hesitation until we were in the dark and then he had my back against the wall.

Threading his fingers through my hair, his mouth caught mine with a frenzied kiss that left me breathless. When he moved his lips off mine, then pressed them against my ear, he whispered, "I've never loved anyone the way I love you."

My heart sped up, and I wrapped my legs around his waist. "Me, too, Alex. I can't believe this is real. It's just too great."

With a few swift movements, he had his jeans undone and pushed his hot, thick manhood into my anticipating womanhood. With him inside me, I felt undeniably stronger. I felt invincible when he and I were joined that way.

Lifting me up and down to stroke his long cock, he growled, "You're always going to be mine, baby. I'm never giving you up."

Elation spread through me at the thought of always being with him. "I'll never let you go either, Alex. My thoroughly sexy man."

As he thrust into me over and over, each stroke he made brought us closer. There, on the side of a Miami nightclub, I realized Alex would always be there for me—with me.

I lavished kisses all over his face, whimpering words of love. I wanted him to feel my immense love. He should have no doubts in his mind about how much he meant to me.

"Hey, who's back there?" A man called out, then flicked on a flashlight, aiming it at us.

"Shit!" Alex said as he backed up away from me after I dropped my feet to the ground.

Quickly I situated myself back into my dress and panties then ran my hands through my hair to tame it a bit. "What should we do?"

"What the hell are you kids doing back there?" the man called out as he came toward us.

"Run," Alex hissed, then grabbed my hand and took off in the opposite direction of the man.

I flew behind him, my feet hardly touching the ground, and I lost one heel, then the other in the chase. The flashlight bounced behind us as the man called out, "Stop!" over and over again.

But Alex wasn't about to stop. We kept going until we came out on the next street over, then we blended into the crowded sidewalk, leaving the man behind.

Gasping for air, I asked, "Can we go back to the bungalow now?"

Alex laughed, then stepped to the curb to hail a cab. "Yes, we can go back now."

Sitting in the backseat of the smelly cab, I leaned against Alex's broad chest, smiling away. "That was exciting!"

He kissed the top of my head. "I've never done anything like that. And nearly getting caught put the icing on the cake."

"I can't believe you ran. You're such an outlaw." I giggled, then looked up into his smile.

His arms wrapped around me. "I couldn't let your name get tarnished, Ky. One day I'll meet your father, and I won't need to hide the fact his daughter was arrested for public indecency. My hopes are for him to respect me."

"So you ran for me?" He nodded. "Cool. I've got myself a real hero, don't I?"

"Nah, I'm not a hero." He kissed my forehead. "It was purely selfish. I've got plans for you someday, and I want to keep your name clean."

"Plus it wouldn't look good if you had a charge like that on your record." He must have considered his medical practice when he ran.

"It was all about was you, baby." He sighed. "Lately, you've taken the number one spot in my mind. If I'm not thinking about you, then it's Tabby. My two girls. I'd do anything for you both."

And I knew he would, too.

I laid my head back on his chest, listening to his heart beating. "I'd do anything for both of you, too, Alex. I love Tabby like she was my own kid."

"I know you do." He moved his hand up and down my arm as his lips pressed against the top of my head. "We make one happy family."

I couldn't wipe the smile off my face. "Do we?"

He nodded, then pulled me closer to kiss me again. Wrapping my arms around his neck, I kissed him back as I moved to sit on his lap. I didn't care if the cab driver would see what we were doing. It was *so* not like me.

Moving my hands between us, I unleashed Alex's beast, then pulled my panties to the side before straddling him. We looked into each other's eyes as I slid down his hard cock.

Alex ran his thumb over my lips. "God, I love you, Kyla Gertrude Rush."

I tried not to let the sound of my middle name throw me off as I moved slowly up and down. "I shouldn't have told you that dreadful name."

"You're supposed to say you love me back, Ky." He moved his hands to my waist, lifting me at the speed he wanted.

I cradled his face in my hands. "I love you more than you will ever understand, Alexander Montgomery Arlen."

All the way back to the bungalow, we rode that way, connected but not trying to get any more than that. As we pulled to a stop near the beach, the driver said, "You'll have to walk from here."

I popped off Alex's lap and he handed the driver a couple of hundred dollar bills. "Thank you, sir. Have a good night."

Smiling, the driver drove away, joyful with his tip. I looped my arm through Alex's as we walked through the sand to get to our beach bungalow. The stars shone so brightly; they looked bigger than they did in Seattle. "It's so beautiful out here tonight. Back home it's raining and cold. Here it's like paradise."

We stopped, and Alex pulled me to sit on the sand with him. "Let's take a minute to look at the night sky."

Looking up, I pointed at the Big Dipper. "I only know that constellation and the Little Dipper near it. I suppose being in the Navy, you know most of them."

"Yeah." He gazed upward. "I was on an Arleigh Burke destroyer. I'd sit on deck sometimes at night, looking at the stars. I'd make wishes on some of them."

I leaned my head on his shoulder as he draped one arm around my shoulders. "What kinds of wishes did you make?"

"Wishes about life and love and finding happiness." He kissed the side of my head. "And they came true, too."

I'd never been happier! "I've never wished for anything like this. I didn't know love like this existed outside of the movies." I looked at one star in particular. "But now I want to wish for this to never end."

Alex chuckled. "Everything ends, Ky. No amount of wishing can change that."

I didn't want to think about endings. Alex had been through an ending; he knew the facts of life and death. "Does it scare you, Alex? The knowledge that all things—all people—end?"

"I've never been the kind of guy who was scared of anything, but I was scared of you. Falling in love with you is what I was scared of."

"Yeah, I know." I looked up and kissed his cheek. "I'm glad you got over that."

"Me, too." He kissed my lips softly. "Living without love just because you're afraid of endings isn't much of a life. This life is not meant to be lived alone. No matter how bad the heart breaks, it can mend itself, given time and patience. I've found that out and have you to thank."

Thinking of how tough it must've been to lose his wife, and at a young age, he managed to overcome that fear. But I was glad he had. "I hope we've got many, many years ahead of us, Alex."

"I do, too, baby." He kissed me again. "Me, too."

17

ALEX

After the most amazing weekend, we got back home a little bit before Tabby's grandparents arrived. When Mr. Randolph headed to the front door just as Ky and I walked in from the garage, he let us know they were there. "Seems your in-laws followed you two."

Ky looked worried. "I'll be upstairs."

"Why?" She seemed to be out of sorts.

"The grandmother doesn't seem to care for me." She pulled her hand, trying to get me to let it go.

"We'll have to fix that, won't we?" I wasn't letting her go and made her come along with me. "She will not hurt you, Ky. Please trust me."

She wasn't taking it well as she whined, "I don't want to. Even just her sole expression makes me feel inadequate."

I totally understood. "Ky, she intimidated me, too. She'll be in our lives; nothing will stop that. Come to terms with that. The same way I have."

"So this is what comes along with loving someone?" She frowned. "I hate this part of love."

Chuckling, I put my arm around her, pulling her closer. "It's not all diamonds and roses, baby."

Meeting my old in-laws in the foyer, I couldn't help but smile as Tabby ran to me. "Daddy!"

I let go of Ky to pick up my eager daughter. "There's my girl! Did you miss me?"

"Yep." She kissed my face. "So much!" Then she held her arms out to Ky. "And you, too!"

Ky took her out of my arms, hugging and kissing her, and that's when I noticed the astonished look my mother-in-law was giving me.

"Hi, Rebecca. How was Tabby?"

"Fantastic as usual." The look faded away as she pulled her tan leather gloves off, laying them across the top of her Gucci purse. "We missed seeing you when we picked her up. How are you holding up?"

There it was, she again tried to pull grief out of me. "I've been great." Turning my attention to my father-in-law. "And how have you been doing, Claus?"

"Fine." He reached out to shake my hand. "We're going to Brussels for a month. We're leaving next week. Can't wait to go. Haven't been there before."

"Sounds nice." I watched Ky put Tabby down, her eyes on the floor. I reached out, pulling her to me and putting my arm around her. "I know you've already met, but we've got news, Ky and I. We're a couple now."

Ky's eyes stayed glued to the floor, and I was glad for that as Rebecca's eyes went wide. "No! What?"

Tabby clapped and jumped up and down. "Oh, yay! You have love!"

Pleased with my daughter's reaction, I wasn't feeling the same way about my mother-in-law's. "Seems not only did I find the perfect person to help me raise Tabby, but I found the perfect person for me, too."

"This is insane, Alexander," Rebecca stamped her petite foot. "I will not stand for this."

Looking at the way Tabby's lips pouted, and Ky's eyes wouldn't leave the floor, it may be best for them to leave the room. "Ky, why don't you take Tabby up and help her unpack her things?"

"Sure." Ky agreed, then picked up Tabby and left me alone with the people who obviously disapproved of my relationship. Which is unacceptable.

Claus ran his hand over his face, upset. "What will Rachelle think of this, Alexander?"

I shouldn't have to point this out, but felt I needed to, "Rachelle won't be affected by this, Claus. She's not here to be hurt by another lover."

Rebecca threw her hands in the air. "This isn't love, Alexander! This is the product of a few years of loneliness, but it's not love. No one falls in love with their much-younger nanny! One might screw the girl, but one does not fall in love with her. Everyone knows that."

The way Claus nodded shook me in a way. "Look, I'm not from your background. I know where you come from and the circles you run in, and people do things differently. But I'm not you. I don't have uppity people in my life to explain things to except for you guys. But you guys aren't really in my life. You're in Tabby's."

"And as Tabitha's grandmother, I must say that this is a travesty, Alexander." Rebecca played her grandmother card far too early in the game to suit me. "She needs a stable person in the role of mother. Not another child. Have you given any thought as to what will happen when this girl needs to sow her wild oats?"

"She's not a teenager, Rebecca." I ran my hand over my face in frustration. "Ky is a mature young woman. She's not like most girls her age. And she loves Tabby. She's a perfect role model for my daughter."

Claus looked at me with one cocked brow. "I'm not so sure about that. Tabitha's grammar isn't what it was. She's picked up a lot of slang."

Rebecca chimed in, "And she's saying only parts of words, like *def* instead of definitely. And *totes* instead of totally. I don't like it. It's not how a Vanderhaven speaks."

"It's fine. Kids talk like that these days. You can't stop her from hearing things like that. Ky isn't the only individual who speaks that way." I knew they'd say something about that. They'd always been so strict about using proper language.

"And just when will you be enrolling Tabitha in a preschool, Alexander?" Claus asked. "She's three now. She should've been in one already."

I didn't want to send her to school yet. "Not that it's any of your business, but I'm not going to send her to preschool until she turns four."

Rebecca did not like me saying it wasn't their business; it was written all over her face. "Now see here, Alexander, Tabitha is *our* granddaughter. We have a responsibility to her. That means she *is* our business. And as such, we don't think it sets a good example for her if you have a relationship with her sitter. What if she grows up to marry a stable boy?"

Laughing, I had to say, "I don't believe they have those anymore, Rebecca."

Waving her hand in the air, she huffed, "You know what I mean."

Claus added, "As one of us, Tabitha is expected to behave in a way that's fitting. And you are, too, Alexander. When you married our daughter, we explained things to you. Don't you remember?"

They had sat me down and told me what was expected of me and what wasn't allowed. But I wasn't a part of that family anymore. "I'm no longer a part of the Vanderhaven family, Claus. And Tabby is an Arlen. She may have your blood running through her veins, but she has mine as well and carries my last name. There's no need for you to worry about her tarnishing the Vanderhaven moniker."

"How simple of you, Alexander," Rebecca said. "As a doctor, you should be smarter than that. Tabitha will always be a Vanderhaven. She's an heiress. Much like her mother, she will be expected to behave like one. And not one of those spoiled ones, either." She turned to look at her husband. "Perhaps we should consider stopping our travels so we can take care of Tabitha?"

"There's no need for that because that's not going to happen." I wasn't about to let them undermine me. "Tabby stays with me. End of discussion."

Neither of them was used to declinations. Claus pointed at the ceiling. "What will Rachelle think about this, Alexander?"

"She's probably mad at you guys for threatening me." What is her father thinking? Did he honestly believe that Rachelle wanted me to be alone—or worse—be with someone of her parent's choosing?

"Rachelle wants us to do what's right for her daughter," Claus went on. "And it's always been to stay with you. Now that you've gone and jumped off the deep end, falling in love with a member of your staff, now we must intervene. It's in Tabitha's best interest to live with us if you continue this idiotic charade of a relationship."

"For your information, Tabby loves being with us both. We've done lots of things together, and she's perfectly comfortable and happy with Ky and me." I shoved my hands into my pockets, fisting them as I started to get angrier about their intrusion into my personal life. "This shouldn't even be happening. I didn't even have to tell you about Ky." Maybe I should've just kept my mouth closed.

Rebecca grinned. "Keep your mouth closed about what you do behind closed doors, and we won't say another word about taking Tabitha away from you. Hide your tawdry things away from our granddaughter and society as a whole. We'll pretend you've never said another word."

Hide the love I've found?

"No way." Not only would that be unfair, but it would devastate Ky. I wanted to be open about what we had. "We're going to be a family. One day in the near future you may even hear Tabby calling Ky *mom*."

Rebecca grabbed her chest, staggering backward. "No!"

Oh, the drama!

Claus caught her as she stumbled back into his waiting arms. Apparently, she's done that on more than one occasion, because he'd gotten right into place.

"Yes," I crossed my arms in front of me. "Ky and I are a couple now. Get over it. She'll be in your granddaughter's life whether you approve or not. My advice to you is to get on board. It might cost you the adoration of your granddaughter if you say nasty things about the woman she loves."

Claus looked at his wife. "She talked a lot about her this weekend."

Rebecca nodded. "She's already got too much influence over Tabitha as it is. If she sees her as a mother figure, all will be lost. We've got to move forward, Claus. For our daughter and granddaughter, we've got to do what's right."

He nodded, and my jaw dropped. "You're not doing anything, Rebecca. You can't. I've never done wrong to my daughter to take her away from me."

"We can cut off your money, Alexander," Claus said. "That was our daughter's inheritance, not yours."

"As her husband, when she passed, her money is mine." It pissed me off he'd use that against me. "Rachelle wanted me to have it. She wanted to keep our daughter's life as similar to what it was before she passed. And the fact you want to take it away from us tells me that Rachelle didn't tell you about the papers she had drawn up that left her assets to me."

Claus looked at his wife. "Did she tell you she'd done anything like that?"

Rebecca shook her head. "I'm sure our lawyers can fix anything she's done." She looked at me with narrowed eyes. "We'll give you a short time to come to your senses, Alexander. Only a short time. Drop the girl or hide the girl, that's your choice." Then she turned away and they walked out of my home.

When I turned back around, I saw Ky standing there with her eyes cast on the floor.

"Baby, don't worry." I walked toward her, and she put up her hands to stop me.

Now what?

18

KY

My hands on his chest, I felt the buzz in my brain as I said the words I'd never thought I would say, "I don't want to see you anymore, Alex."

"You don't mean that," he whispered as he took my hands off his chest, holding them between us.

"Tabby is more important than anything else." Her grandparents had more money and power than Alex. "Those people can make things happen that you can't. They can take her if they want to. And you don't care about the money, but I'm sure their lawyers can take that away, too. You've got too much to lose to keep things the way they are between us."

"I'm not afraid, Ky." He pulled me in closer, wrapping his arms around me. "That's not entirely true. I am afraid of losing you. I won't lose you over them and their idle threats. So get that through your head right now."

I held on to him, not wanting to let him go, but knowing I should. "They're the first people in a long line that'll declare what you're doing with me is dimwitted."

"I think you're wrong." He rocked from side to side with me. "*This* isn't dense. Not even a little. My colleagues don't think anything bad about this. I see those people every day. And here's a tidbit about myself, Ky: I don't give a damn what other people think. If my old inlaws want to take Rachelle's money, then so be it. I make plenty of money on my own anyhow."

"But this house," I whined thinking about him and Tabby losing the home they lived in. "You'd lose it all."

"No, I wouldn't." He hugged me tighter. "Everything we have is paid for. The house, the cars, everything. So what would I lose? Access to billions is all. And I doubt that'll even happen. Rachelle used her parents' lawyers to draw up the will. So their threat isn't even doable." His lips pressed against the top of my head. "But I'd give up all the money in the world if it meant I'd get to keep you."

I didn't know what to do. So I pushed him back a bit to look into his eyes. "Promise me that if they take you to court, and they are able to take Tabby away, you will end things with me." The pain I felt at having that looming over us was ungodly.

"It won't happen that way," he said. "We don't have to come up with a plan. They're upset right now. They'll learn to accept it. Besides, they don't have time to raise a kid. They barely had time for Rachelle. She lived at boarding schools most of her childhood."

I shivered thinking of Tabby living in one of those places. "That would be dreadful if Tabby had to go through that." He needed to know I would walk away from him before anything bad happened to Tabby. "You might not need a plan if the worst happens, but I do. Understand that I will leave you if it looks like they'll get Tabby. I mean it, Alex."

He smiled, then kissed me. "You really love her."

I put my head on his shoulder as I hugged him. "As much as I love you. You guys are like family to me."

"You'll make a great mother." He kissed me again. "Someday. When we're ready."

My breath caught in my throat. "Are you saying one day you and I will have a kid?" A chill that flashed through my body.

"Or kids. A few more would enhance this family." He twirled me around in a circle, dancing with me to no music. "You're my family,

Ky. No one can break my family up. Not even the old, rich Vanderhavens."

Tabby came running into the foyer, her arms wrapped around my legs. Alex let me go to pick her up, then hugged me again. "Get in on this, Tabby. We're in love and love you, too."

She put her hand on my cheek, then whispered, "I love you, too."

Tears were stabbing the backs of my eyes. "Me, too. I'd do anything for you, Tabby."

"Can we have pizza?" she asked. "Nana only has veggies."

I thought about how her life would be if her grandparents did manage to take her away. "Pizza sounds like a great idea. You must be starving."

She rubbed her tummy. "Yes."

Alex looked at his daughter with a sad expression. "Did you not have a good time with your grandparents, Tabby?"

"I missed here." Tabby hugged him, and he looked at me weirdly.

Putting her down, he said, "Go put on a coat and we'll go to the pizza place."

She ran off like a streak of lightning as Alex looked at me. "I might need to draw up papers for you sometime, too."

I had no idea what he was talking about. "For what?"

"For you to be able to keep Tabby if anything ever happens to me." He looked concerned. "And you'd keep her capital, too. Until she's old enough to handle it on her own." He bit his lower lip as he contemplated things. "She needs to be protected. I don't want her to grow up the way Rachelle did. She complained about her upbringing a lot. I don't want my daughter to go through all that nonsense they put her mother through."

"What about your parents, Alex?" I had no idea if he could make this stick if anything did happen to him, which I didn't even want to think about. But losing his wife to cancer had him considering things I didn't want to.

He shook his head. "Tabby hasn't seen them much. She doesn't know them enough to be her guardians. She wouldn't do well with her other grandparents raising her." His eyes met mine. "Would you want that responsibility, Ky?"

"To be honest, it would kill me for someone to take her away from me." But I didn't have it in me to fight her mother's parents. "The legal papers would have to be pretty much bulletproof. The Vanderhavens seem to be tough adversaries. It would better to have them on our side."

"It would," he agreed. "Maybe with time, they will see we're not so bad."

Even he didn't want to fight them. But he would do a lot better job than I could. "Let's pray nothing ever happens to you, Alex."

Looking into my eyes, he didn't seem convinced. "If only prayers could stop bad things from happening, baby." He put his arm around me as we heard Tabby running back to us.

"I'm ready, Daddy." She skidded to a stop, then took her father's hand.

Heading to the garage, we stopped off at the kitchen. Alex looked at the food the chef was already preparing. "We're taking Tabby out for pizza. Ky and I will be eating dinner here though. We'll take it in the lounge. Tabby's weekend was *sans* junk food, and she has a craving."

Rudy smiled at Tabby. "When you get back home, I'll serve you up a big piece of the chocolate cake I made."

"You miss me, Mr. Rudy?" Tabby asked with a grin.

"I did." Rudy tapped his finger to her nose. "And those cute little freckles of yours, too." He reached into his pants pocket and pulled out a five dollar bill. "Here, play some games on me, Princess."

With wide eyes, Tabby took the money. "Thank you, Mr. Rudy." She looked up at her dad, then at me. "What a great day!"

Alex looked at me. "Yeah, it sure is." As we walked away, he leaned in close to whisper in my ear, "And what a night we'll have, my sweet little thing." He looked over his shoulder. "Rudy, can you tell Chloe to get Ky's things moved out of her room and into mine while we're out?"

"I see," Rudy said with a smirk as I blushed. "Congrats, you guys. You make a beautiful couple."

Tabby seemed to think the same way, "They are cute."

Alex beamed as I laid my head on his shoulder. He'd been right about the people around us being okay with us. That was what really mattered.

As I helped Tabby get secured in her car seat, Alex got behind the wheel of his Suburban. "So, which pizza place is it going to be, Tabby?"

"Hobbit's Pizza." She reached out to run her fingers through my hair. "Your hair is shiny. Pretty."

"Thank you. Your hair looks pretty today, too." What I overheard her grandparents saying about her grammar? I better start watching how I spoke and correct her when she used poor grammar. "You know, if you hear me saying anything like *totes* or *def* or anything like that, remind me that it's not proper to speak that way. I'll do the same for you. We do want to be smart, don't we?"

Nodding, she agreed. "I want to be smart."

"Good." I finished buckling her in, then got in the front seat, finding Alex smiling at me. "What?"

"You make me happy." He pushed the button to lift the garage door then backed out.

Tabby pointed at the radio. "Can we hear music, Dad? I missed my music."

We both laughed, and I turned on the Disney music channel, and we all sang along as we went down the road.

This is beginning to feel a lot more special.

19

ALEX

The activities at the pizza place had worn Tabby out. She'd fallen asleep in the car, and I carried her straight up to bed. After tucking her in, I stopped by my bedroom to make sure Ky's things had been moved into it. Seeing her robe hanging on the hook on the outside of the second closet made my heart dance. "She's officially moved in." I closed the door, then went down to meet Ky in the lounge where we'd be served dinner.

She sat at the bar, sipping on something pink. Her eyes followed me as I approached her. "Want to taste?"

"It looks kind of fruity." I wrinkled my nose.

"It's got rose tequila in it." She handed the glass to me. "Come on, taste it."

Taking a little sip, I found it good enough. "Not bad."

"I made it up myself. I'm going to call it Ky's Rose." She smiled as she placed the short glass on the bar. "It's got the tequila I told you about, a drop of maraschino cherry juice, and a splash of triple sec."

"You're getting quite creative, aren't you?" I rubbed her shoulders as I stood in front of her, then urged her to sit with me at a table.

Delia came in with our salads. Her eyes went wide as she saw us like that. "Oh, that's what Rudy was hinting at. You two are a couple now?"

Dropping her head, Ky blushed as the chef's assistant learned about us, "We are officially a couple." I took Ky by the chin to pull her pretty face up. "Right, baby?"

She giggled. "Right. We're a great thing."

"It's nice to see you happy," Delia said. "Things will work out well for you both. I'll bring the grilled swordfish in later. Enjoy."

I took Ky to the table, pulling a chair out for her. As she took the seat, she made a little moaning noise as she said, "Yum, swordfish. How ritzy."

"That moan made has me hungry for something else." I sat down, then reached across the table, taking her hand and holding it as I looked into those pools of green and brown. "I checked the bedroom after putting Tabby down. Your things have been moved to *our* bedroom now. And I am ready to break that bed in with you."

Smiling, Ky looked away. "This is too much. At first it felt like a dream. I'm kind of freaking out."

"Don't." I pulled her hand up, leaving a kiss on top. "This is real, Ky. All of it. Things won't always go as planned. We will have disagreements."

She cocked her head to one side. "Okay, now that we'll be sharing a bathroom, you should know that my mother trained my father well. We never had to deal with a toilet seat being left up. I tend to go into the bathroom at night without turning on a light, trusting I won't have a splashdown event."

I let her hand go to snap my fingers. "Dang it. I never put that seat down," I joked.

"Well, you better start, or you'll hear me screaming for you to come rescue me." She laughed, then took a bite of her salad. "Oh wow. Raspberry vinaigrette. It's amazing."

I took a bite and agreed, "It is tasty."

After a scrumptious dinner, we headed to our room. It felt good to share a room with someone I love. As we walked into the living area of the suite, I gestured to the room. "I want you to give this space your personal touch. This is home to you."

"The first thing would be a television." She smiled as she took my hand, pulling me out of the living area and into the bedroom. "We can binge-watch shows while eating ice cream and drinking wine. That sounds like what couples do together on a Saturday night, doesn't it? I've never been a couple, so I'm just spit-balling here."

"We can do that sometimes." I pulled her into my arms. "But mostly I'd like to ravage your body while we're in here."

"That sounds good, too." She ran her hands up my arms, then into my hair. "How about we start ravaging each other right now?"

"I like the way you think, baby." Pulling her shirt off, I tossed it on the floor. "And no getting up to change the sheets or pick up the things we're tossing off got it?"

She nodded as she took my shirt off and threw it across the room. "Got it."

The bed in my room was an Alaskan King, much bigger than the queen size she slept in. One glance at the bed and she was bewildered. She would feel lost in the thing. "Don't worry, Ky. I'll hang onto you, so you don't get lost on our enormous bed."

"Promise?" she asked, laughing as she shucked out of her jeans. "Cause I can see myself winding up at the foot of this bed clear across the other side."

"I won't let you get far away from me." I dropped my drawers, too, and looked at her gloriously naked body as she scanned mine. "First night in our room. It feels right."

She nodded, then climbed up on the bed on her knees. "It does feel right. Now come over here and climb up on this monstrosity with me and make me feel even more right." Turning over, she moved up the bed on her hands and knees to get to the top.

I yanked her by the ankle, stopping her. "And where do you think you're going?" I dragged her back to me, smacking her ass once.

"Hey!" she yelped.

Flipping her onto her back, I pulled her until her ass was perched at the edge of the bed. Getting on my knees, I blew air across her cunt, then flicked my tongue out to tease her clit. She made a mewling sound that made my cock jerk. "I'm going to get my dessert now. You just lie back and let me eat you all up. I've got a craving for another drink. This one doesn't have liquor to intoxicate me."

Pressing my lips to her more intimate ones, I grazed them over her before running my tongue through the hot folds. She took my hair in her hands, pulling it as she groaned, "Yes, baby. Oh, that feels so good."

"You taste like Heaven, baby." I licked her up and down, then pressed my tongue into her sweet pussy, using it to fuck her relentlessly until she was crying in her orgasm.

Whimpering as she tugged my hair, she asked, "Will you fuck me, please?"

Getting up, my cock yearned to be inside of her now quaking walls. "Since you've asked so nicely." I held her legs apart as I stood in front of her then thrust my hard cock into her pulsing pussy.

"Oh, yeah!" She grabbed the sheets in both hands as I held her hips and made hard thrusts.

Watching my cock slide in and out of her, I felt mesmerized. Slick and shiny, my cock buried itself inside of her, then pulled back out. Her clit took my attention as it swelled, and I used one finger to massage it. It got even bigger, then she was moaning again, and her body came all over my dick with a clenching action and more juices flowed.

Pulling my cock out of her, I inserted two fingers into her, then pulled them out, coating them with our combined secretions. Tasting them myself, I found it too good not to share and dipped them again, then put my fingers into her mouth. She sucked them as she moaned. Climbing up on the bed, I put my cock, still glistening with those combined juices, to her sweet lips.

Opening her mouth, I moved my dick into it, then leaned over to place my hands on the bed to hold myself up. With a humping motion, I fucked her mouth with slow, steady movements as I held her arms down with my knees.

Helpless to stop me, Ky moaned with ecstasy as I kept going, easing a bit further down her throat until I could bury my cock all the way inside of her mouth. "Fuck, baby. Take it all. Shit, you're so good at this. Damn, I can't believe you're mine."

I moved faster and a little harder as I fucked her that way. But then I felt the urge to come and had to pull out. I didn't want to climax in her mouth. I wanted to come somewhere I'd never came yet.

She wiped her mouth with the back of her hand as I rolled off her. Smiling, Ky said, "That was different."

"Did you like it?" I asked as I stuck my cock back into her to get it all gelled up with her natural juices.

She nodded. "It was pretty intense being held down like that. I felt like I was your captive. I liked it."

Pulling back out of her, I twirled my finger. "Okay, on your hands and knees. Then drop down until your shoulders are on the bed. I'm going to pop this tight little ass of yours."

She turned her head to look at me over her shoulder. "You're going to stick it up my ass?"

Nodding, I couldn't help but smile as she licked her lips. "Well, this ought to be something."

I decided to grab her a pillow in case she needed to make a lot of noise. "Here." I placed the pillow in front of her. "If you feel like screaming."

Her eyes went wide. "Do you think it'll hurt?"

"I have no idea. I've never done this." I shrugged. "Another first for both of us? I like the idea of sharing this with you."

"Yeah, me, too." She wiggled her ass. "And spank me! I don't know why that rocks my world the way it does."

Smacking her ass, I gave her several sharp slaps with one hand while plunging one finger into her cunt to get it wet before pushing it into her asshole. It didn't go in far at all, then I remembered something medical school had taught me. "Push like you're trying to poop, Ky."

She looked back at me. "Gross."

"Just trust me." I kept my finger right where it was, and when she made a little grunting sound and pushed, my finger slipped all the way in, then I moved it back and forth.

"Oh," she moaned. "Oh, yeah."

"It feels good?" I asked as I kept pumping it.

"Yeah, it does." She looked at me over her shoulder again. "Hey, put your dick in there and smack me as you fuck me. Tell me I'm your dirty little slut. I'm getting off on the captive role playing. You're my sexy kidnapper who is tormenting me with pleasure."

"I can be that." I pulled my finger out, then pushed my cock back into her soaked pussy to lubricate it before I put the tip at her butthole again. "Okay, push again, baby."

She did, and then buried her face in the pillow as I slipped into her virgin hole. The tightness was insane as I plunged in. I wouldn't last long. "Oh, shit, you're tight!"

Finally, she stopped screaming and lifted her face off the pillow. "Now it's better. That was rough at first."

"This is amazing." I slammed into her ass, smacking her on the side of her buttock once in a while. "You've got no idea. There are ripples that make my cock feel a way it's never felt before." And then she pushed again and clenched even tighter around me. "Fuck!" I exploded into her; stars flashed in my eyes as I came hard.

Shit, I love this girl!

20

KY

A week later and the honeymoon phase still hadn't gone away. But work came for Alex.

We hadn't heard a word from Tabby's grandparents, and I thought Alex had been right about them needing time to take everything in. Tabby met my parents earlier that day, and they would come over to meet my guy very soon.

I sat at the dining room table, making a list of foods my parents liked. Rudy asked me to do that so he could cater to them.

Steven came into the dining room with a coloring book in his hand. "Tabby left this in the car. I thought she might want it."

"She's napping right now." I tapped the table. "Leave it here, please."

He put the book on the table. "Your parents are kind, Ky. I don't get invited in very often. And the coffee was good, too."

"I'm glad you liked it. Mom's not one to leave anyone sitting outside." I smiled. "You're about the same age as Alex. I haven't heard about a significant other. Are you unattached?"

"I am indeed." He looked timid. "I've had some issues with PTSD. It's got me not wanting to inflict myself on others."

"Are you getting help for that?" I hoped he wasn't trying to get through that all on his own.

"Yeah." He nodded. "I've been seeing a therapist for the last three years. He's helping me a lot. He was in the Army years ago and knows what it's like to see things a person was never meant to see."

"Three years is a pretty good amount of time." He did not need to be alone forever. "If you want, I could throw a small party here sometime. I've got lots of friends. Some are very pretty."

Laughing, he said, "I wouldn't have an aversion to joining a party with pretty girls in attendance."

"Cool." I made a mental note to talk to Alex about having a party. "I'll start making plans."

"Sounds good." He hooked his thumb back, gesturing to the door he'd come through. "I've got some things to do. See ya later, Ky."

"Later, Steven." I got back to working on my list thinking it looked pretty bland. Mom liked flounder, so she'd love swordfish. Drawing a line through that, I replaced it with a more grand fish. And I drew another line through hamburger steaks, replacing it with filet mignon.

My cell vibrated in my pocket, and I pulled it out to see Alex's name on the screen. "Hey, Babe."

"Hi there, gorgeous," he greeted me. "How about you bring Tabby down to eat dinner with me here at the hospital? They're flying a patient in, and I'll be late getting home."

I couldn't hide the disappointment, "Aw, man."

"I know," he commiserated. "Have Rudy pack up dinner, and we'll eat it in the cafeteria. Is an hour from now okay?"

"Your daughter is napping. I'd hate to wake her up." I thought about how much she'd been growing lately. "She's a whole inch taller than the last time. All that growing means she needs more rest. But she could stay here with Chloe if she's not awake by then."

"At least I'd see one of my girls," he said. "I'll see you then, my love."

"See you soon." I got up and went into the kitchen to inform Rudy of the change in plans. "Alex called. A patient is flying in and he won't be home for dinner. He wants you to pack it up and send it with me. We're having a picnic in the hospital's cafeteria."

"I'll grab the camping plates and utensils," Rudy said as he headed to the pantry. "Should I put in a bottle of wine for you guys?"

"Depends on what you've made." I leaned over the island bar to see what he was working on.

"Roasted game hens with squash and kumquat stuffing. A white wine is what I was going to serve it with." He held up some wine glasses he'd pulled out of the pantry and waved them in the air.

"I don't see why you shouldn't send the wine you've picked out. Just make sure to put the corkscrew in, please." I turned around as I heard the house phone ringing. "Now, that doesn't happen much."

Rudy nodded. "Chloe will get it, she always does."

"I'm going to go freshen up for the trip to the hospital and see if I can rouse Tabby to come along." I left the kitchen, making my way to the stairs when Chloe came out of the main living area.

She looked right at me. "You've got a call, Ky. You can take it in there if you'd like."

"Who is it?" I felt uneasy as I'd never given anyone the house number.

Ducking her head, she kept moving. "The Vanderhavens."

"Shit," I said under my breath.

My feet barely moved as I didn't want to speak to them. Nor did I understand why they'd call me instead of Alex. If they had to know anything about their granddaughter, they should to talk to him anyway.

When I got to the phone that lay on the coffee table, I stared at it for a moment before getting the courage to pick it up. "This is Ky."

"This is Mr. Vanderhaven," Tabby's grandfather said. "Look, I'm not trying to be mean to you, Kyla. We've done our research and have found that we can't use Rachelle's inheritance to get Alexander do as we wish."

I was glad to hear that. "So, you've decided to drop the whole issue?"

"Oh, Heaven's no." He went so far as to laugh as if the idea was ludicrous. "No, we've come up with something else. Something that pertains to you and only you, Kyla Gertrude Rush. We've had your background checked."

I had nothing to hide. "And you found it to be clean."

"Oh, yes, we have found it spotless." He cleared his throat. "So we came up with this idea to give you something as your family has very little money. No savings at all. Did you know that, Ky? They have no savings at all. And your father's retirement money has been borrowed on. I don't know how he or your mother will ever retire. And once you reach seventy, your opportunities are pretty much over."

"I can help them out when that time comes." What is he was getting at? "I make plenty of money, and almost all is available to them when the time comes."

"You're talking about the fifteen thousand you have in your checking account?"

He knew that? "And just how did you find out all this financial information?"

"I've got ways. And I've got ways to make those numbers grow in not only your account but that of your parents as well."

"Why would you do that, Mr. Vanderhaven?" He was talking in circles.

"We love our granddaughter, Kyla. We only want what's best for her. And, like I said before, I don't want to hurt you." He paused before going on, "The fact is you're not good for our granddaughter. That said, I'm going to make you an offer you can't refuse."

"Bet I can." I put my hand on my hip as anger filled me.

"If you truly care for Tabitha, you will accept this offer," he said. "She deserves better, and you know that."

Feeling as if I had the wind knocked out of me, I fell back to sit on the sofa behind me. "I love her, sir. I adore her. I would lay down my life for her. So, please tell me how much better she could get?"

He had an answer, "Tabitha needs someone affluent raising her and who knows how to act accordingly. You've grown up nearly destitute. The things you will accept are not things a person as special as Tabitha should. She needs a better role model. It's not personal, Kyla. Would you have a maid raising a rich man's child?"

What did he think I'd say? I said what was in my heart, "If that maid loved that child as if it were her own, then yes, I would have a maid raise a rich man's child. I've made a family here, sir. Sorry you don't believe anyone so young and poor could do such a thing, but I have. I came into this home, and I filled the emptiness your daughter left with her passing. It might not be exactly the way she would've done things, but both Tabby and Alex are happy. That's because of me. You want me to take that happiness away from them? Again? They've already lost the mother and wife Rachelle was to them. Are they to lose me, too?"

"You make an excellent argument, I'll give you that," he condoned. "But you're not mature enough to know who you'll be once that occurs. I'm sorry. Again, this isn't personal."

How much more personal it could get? "You want me to leave the people I love, Mr. Vanderhaven? And they love me. That's pretty damn personal."

"Oh, language, please," he said. "I hate to hear dirty words come out of a woman's mouth."

"Then perhaps you should hang up." I had a ton of words ready to rip through my lips, and each one was aimed at him.

"Perhaps you should hear me out," he said. "I will give you a million dollars. I will give your mother another million dollars. And I will give your father a million dollars. All you need to do is move out of Seattle. Do not let Alexander know where you are. Leave him and our granddaughter behind, Kyla. You will only bring them both down if you stay. At least this way, you will leave with some money in not only your bank but those of your parents too. Leave tonight and the bank accounts will be filled by noon tomorrow. I don't know how long to keep this offer on the table. We will do whatever we have to, Kyla. This is the only way to get out of it unscathed."

Unscathed?

Who the hell is he kidding? Leaving the people I love would scathe the hell out of me.

21

ALEX

After receiving a text from Ky, I headed to the cafeteria where she was waiting with dinner. Walking down the long hallway, I found myself smiling, happy that I'd get to see my girls for a bit.

I couldn't recall a time I'd been so happy about such simple things. Life felt different, and I wasn't about to take one second with Ky and Tabby for granted.

As soon as I went through the doors to the cafeteria, I spotted Ky sitting at a table alone. "Tabby wouldn't wake up?" I asked her, drawing her attention.

"Huh?" She looked up at me with eyes filled with dread. "Oh, Tabby? Yeah, she's still sleeping. Chloe has the baby monitor to get her when she wakes up. She'll text me when she wakes up."

Leaning in, I kissed her cheek. "I'm glad you came." I took the seat across from her and looked at the meal. "So, little chickens for dinner?"

"Game hens, and the stuffing has squash and kumquats." She pulled out a bottle of white wine. "And he added this."

"I can't drink that. I have surgery coming up, remember?"

She put the unopened bottle back in the bag. "Oh, yeah. Well, I've got bottles of water, too." She put two bottles on the table.

Ky was off, anyone who knew her could see that. "Okay, something's going on. Tell me, Ky."

Her hazel eyes, now more brown than green, looked into mine. "I don't know how to say this."

What could be so bad that she felt unable to converse? We had remarkable communications skills. Or so I'd thought. "Baby, you can say anything in the world to me." I thought better about that. "Except that we're through. I won't listen to any of that." I smiled as I reached over to take her hand, drawing it up to kiss her palm.

With a sigh, she said quietly, "Your old father-in-law called me on your house phone."

Instantly, I became agitated. "Why?"

"He had an offer." She looked away, a frown curving her lips. "Not that I entertained it, but he made an offer most people wouldn't refuse." Her eyes came back to mine. "The thing is, he doesn't realize how much I love you and Tabby. He thinks money can buy me off and send me away from the two people I love most."

Suddenly, I realized her hand was in a bad grip. Letting it go, I ran my hands through my hair. "Sorry about the tight grasp, babe. But this has me pretty fucking pissed. What did Claus offer?"

"A million dollars each for my mother, father, and myself." Ky looked at me with a blank expression. "He knew how much money was in all of our accounts. He knew my father borrowed against his retirement account. He knew things he shouldn't have known."

"That man has his ways." I fisted my hands, wanting to punch something. "Although illegal, he's got people who do things for him. Did he have anything else to say?"

She nodded. "He wanted us to take the money and leave town for good." Her hand crept across the table to run over the backs of my knuckles, now white with pressure. "He actually wanted me to leave without saying a thing to you. Tell me how I could do that to someone I love?"

"You couldn't." Releasing the fist I'd made, I took her hand once again. "Don't worry about money. I'd never let your parents sink financially."

Nodding, Ky smiled. "I know that, Alex. It's just that I don't want to be the person who starts a war between you and Tabby's grandparents."

Oh, hell no!

"Listen to me. Stay with us." I wouldn't let the Vanderhavens chase the woman I love out of my life. "I'll deal with those people. Don't worry one tiny bit. When I'm through with them, they'll quit this shit, or they'll be the ones knocked out of Tabby's life."

She shook her head. "Please don't do that, Alex. I don't want Tabby to lose grandparents who love her, just because of me. They're all she has left of her mother."

"Then they need to mind their granddaughter as much as you do, Ky." Her selflessness was beyond compare. "I *will* take care of this. I promise you. I'll try my best to keep them in Tabby's life. But I won't let them bribe or threaten you."

Looking relieved, she grinned. "You're such a hero, Alex."

"No, I'm just a guy who loves his girls." I kissed her hand again. "I love you more than you can possibly understand, Ky. I'm never giving you up. I don't care who disapproves." I wasn't going to let the love I'd finally found go.

Ky couldn't stop smiling as she looked into my eyes. "I'm pretty lucky. It's funny how I never thought love could be like this. I was meant for you, Alex. I was born just for you."

My heart pounded as I thought of what she said. *Born just for me.*

"I have no idea if that's the truth, but now that I have you, you will always be mine." I wasn't about to let that girl go—not ever.

Pointing at the food on the plates in front of us, she said, "We better eat before this stuff gets too cold. Rudy worked hard on it."

Nodding, I let her hand go and started eating. Purposely, I let the subject go. It made me mad to think about it.

We just finished eating when her cell dinged, and she looked at the message. "Tabby's up. I better get going." She packed up all the food and picnic supplies into the basket.

Kissing her goodbye, I held her in my arms for a moment. "I

love you, Kyla. I truly do. Don't let anything anyone else ever says come between us."

She ran her fingertips along my jawline. "I promise you. I love you, too, Alex."

One last kiss, then I had to let her be on her way. Watching her leave, I sighed and felt my heart racing as I thought about Claus.

Taking a walk, I pulled out my cell, calling the man who threatened not only my happiness but Tabby's as well. When the phone rang three times, I knew he was hesitating to answer, but then he finally did, "Alexander."

"Claus, I heard you called Ky today. That was a monumental mistake."

"She told you?" his voice etched with displeasure. "Damn."

"Look, you're doing this in what you believe is Tabby's best interest." They didn't mean to hurt their granddaughter. "But you don't seem to understand how much Tabby loves Ky. And Ky loves her, too. It might hurt you to hear this, but you need to understand. Rachelle couldn't be the mother Tabby needed. She was too sick to be what our baby needed. Now that Ky has come along and more than filled the void, well, I don't want Tabby to lose what she's found in Ky."

His voice had a load of concern in it as he said, "Alexander, our daughter couldn't fulfill her role as mother or wife in the last few years. And Tabitha thinks highly of her nanny. That said, Kyla is not the right person to fill the role of mother to Tabitha. No matter what hold you have on the girl, you're wrong. She's young." He hesitated. "Kyla was an innocent girl until she came to work for you. I had her background checked and sent someone to speak with her old roommates. That girl was a virgin when you met her."

Fury filled me. "You sent someone to get Ky's secrets out of her friends?" That was going way too far. "That's it, Claus. That. Is. It. You can't do anything like this again. Do you understand? I'll turn you into the police for violating all sorts of privacy laws."

"You won't win," he informed me. "My people are discreet. Her roommates won't even know what you're talking about. It was done covertly."

I had it with the man and let him know, "Claus, I can't take this anymore. Frankly, I don't have to."

"Because of Tabitha, you do," he let me know. "There are grandparents' rights, too, you know. We won't be left out of our granddaughter's life. We will never be left out. Nothing can stop that."

"And there's nothing you can do to stop me from living my life and keeping Ky." There were so many things to straighten out between my old in-laws and me. "Claus, the last thing I want to do is fight with you guys. Just leave Ky alone, and things will be fine."

He pulled out the big guns, "Alexander, you're thinking with your dick instead of your brilliant brain. I hate to see this happening to you. I don't think the girl has done this. Your loneliness has. One day you will wake up and wonder what the hell you're doing. She's not only young, but she's a nobody."

I always hated how Rachelle's parents thought you were no one unless you managed to accumulate large amounts of money. "Need I remind you that you haven't earned money on your own, Claus? You were *born* into wealth. You're no better than anyone else. Ky isn't a nobody. No one is a nobody."

"How wrong you are, Alexander. One day, you will see." He wasn't about to give in.

"I hope one day it will be you and Rebecca who sees that Ky isn't just a person passing through our lives. She's here to stay, Claus. Get used to it or get out of our lives." Ky didn't want me to toss Tabby's grandparents out of her life, but I had no choice.

We'd be better off without them if they couldn't accept Ky as part of the family.

22

KY

Weeks went by, and things got quiet on Tabby's grandparents' end. Alex thought they'd gone on a trip and put things behind them, but only for the time being. I didn't care as long as no one was getting in our business.

Walking through the park, Alex and I watched Tabby's eyes light up as she saw the playground. "Yeah!" Taking off like a flash, she headed for the swings where other children were playing.

Letting go of my hand, Alex sprinted after her, scooping her up before she ran into one of the swings. "Hey, you. You've got to watch out for those swings. Those things can hit you and knock you down, baby girl." He kissed her on the forehead. "Besides, there is a tree I'd like us to be under when I ask you something."

Catching up to him, I wondered what kind of a question he had to ask his daughter and why there was a certain tree he needed to ask her under. But I didn't want to butt into his business with her. "The weather is gorgeous today," I said instead.

Still holding Tabby as we walked along the pathway, he looked up at the blue, cloudless sky. "It's the most perfect day. We don't have many of these in Seattle." Then his eyes came to mine. "It feels special today. Don't you think?"

It felt great being outdoors, so I nodded. "Yeah. It's a special sort of day."

"One of those days you'll remember for a long time," he went on. "Maybe even forever?"

I didn't know about all that. "It's a nice day. The temperature is perfect. The sky seems bluer." Taking the time to really take in my surroundings, I took notice of the chirps of the birds, the buzzing insects, and the laughs of the children playing on the playground. "It even sounds nice, too."

"Every living creature seems to be out and having the time of their lives," Alex added. "The atmosphere is almost electric, but surrounded by calmness. I've never seen such a perfect day in a long time."

I couldn't help but laugh at Alex's enthusiasm. "Well aren't you in top spirits today, babe?"

He put one arm around me as he stopped underneath a large oak tree that looked to be hundreds of years old. "I *am* in top spirits, baby." His ice-blue eyes shone brightly in the diminished sunlight. "I've never felt so alive and optimistic."

"Optimistic?" I asked. "About what?"

He shrugged. "About everything. Life in general." He kissed Tabby on the cheek, then put her down. When he got down on one knee in front of her, holding her little hands in his, I looked on with curiosity. "Tabby, have you liked how our lives have changed since Ky came to live with us?"

I held my breath, wondering what would happen if she said no.

Tabby smiled and laughed as she looked up at me, then back at her daddy. "Daddy, I like Ky. She's nice and fun, too. I love Ky."

The way his smile moved over his handsome face lit up his eyes. "I love her too, Tabby."

My legs started to weaken as he kept looking at Tabby instead of me. My heart began to race and pounded so loudly that I could hear it. But still, my lips were pressed together tightly.

"Daddy, are you going to cry?" Tabby asked as she peered into his eyes.

He didn't acknowledge the question. Instead, he asked her another , "Tabby, would you like it if you could call Ky *Mom*?"

For a moment she just looked at him,, then smiled and shook her head. "I want to call her mom."

I clutched my chest.

Is Alex going to ask me to marry him?

Stumbling backward, I stopped when my back hit the tree. When Alex ran his hand over Tabby's head, she stood up, coming over to me. He let go of Tabby's hand, then whispered, "Wish me luck, Tabby."

She clapped her hands and ran in place. "Good luck, Daddy!"

I couldn't breathe, think, or make any sense of anything. When Alex got on one knee in front of me, then pulled out a black box, I nearly passed out. "Kyla Gertrude Rush, I've loved you since I met you. You stole my heart right from the start. I can't think of spending even one day without you in it. My daughter loves you, I love you, so why don't we make this legit and permanent? Will you do me the honor of becoming my wife?"

The earth moved beneath my feet, and I was on my knees in front of Alex, my hands over my mouth and tears making my vision blurred. The sound of Tabby's sweet, little voice brought me out of the stupor, "Say yes! Say yes!"

Gasping, I let my answer fly out of my mouth, "Yes! Yes, Alex!"

Pulling the ring out of the box, he slipped it on my trembling finger. "You've made me happier than I've ever been."

I couldn't take it anymore, with the weight of that ring on my finger, I knew it was official. "Oh, my God!" I threw my arms around him, hugging him so tightly, then I felt tiny arms embracing me from behind, and I let Alex go so I could take Tabby into my arms.

She buried her face in my chest. "You're my mommy!"

Blinking, I tried to stop the tears so I could see Alex's face. And I saw tears streaming down his cheeks as well as he looked at his daughter and me. "This is so much more than I ever expected." He wiped his eyes with the back of his hand. "Damn, I should've done this in the privacy of our house."

Reaching out with my freed-up arm, I took him into the hug. "Come here, Daddy. Get in on this family hug."

This was the best thing to ever happen to me. Being married to Alex hadn't even been a blip on my radar.

I heard a woman clear her throat. "I hate to interrupt."

Alex and I exchanged confused expressions as we let each other go to see who'd said that. Alex asked, "And you are?"

She waved her cell phone at us. "I was taking a walk when I saw you. I stopped and decided I should video this instant for you. How beautiful!"

Getting up off my knees, I thanked her. "Oh, how brilliant! We'll have this moment to look back on forever."

"Give me your number. I'll send the video over." She smiled. "It was presumptuous of me to take it. Something told me to do it, though."

Alex nodded. "I'm glad you did. It's the best gift anyone has ever given us."

Minutes later, we watched the video. "Aw. We're all so in love," Tabby giggled.

She was right; we were all in love. Blood or not, I loved that little girl. "I truly love you, Tabby. I always will. And I can't wait until you call me Mom."

"After the wedding," Alex said. "Then we'll all be Arlens."

Wrapping his arm around me, he took Tabby by the hand, and we headed back to the car in the parking lot. "What a day." I looked at my ring, watching the sun glisten off the large diamond that was surrounded by several smaller ones. "This ring is so beautiful; it's got me lost for words." I never expected something so huge and stunning to be on my finger. But there it was, sparkling. I'd never been dazzled before, but that had to have been what I felt as I looked at that rock on my finger.

Alex kissed the side of my head. "What do you say to stopping off for a nice dinner? I made reservations for us. I kind of had the idea you'd say yes to my proposal. I wanted to end the day with a special feast."

"What haven't you thought of?" I kissed his cheek. "A superb day in the park. The best question I've ever been asked. And now a special dinner? How can things get any better than this?"

The way his eyes held mine... There would be days just as great as this one. As long as we had each other, there would be many days like this one. I knew it, and so did Alex.

Later, as we sat in the restaurant having dinner, Alex brought up a valid point, "Ky, why not introduce me to your parents now that we're engaged?"

Time had gotten away from me, it seemed. "Oh, Alex! Sorry I haven't invited them over yet. They've met Tabby already. Let's do something this weekend. And what about your family? Invite them over, too!" I began to get excited. "This will be great! My parents will meet you as my fiancée!"

I have a fiancée!

It seemed like an eternity since I first met Alex and Tabby—like they'd always been around. Had I been waiting for him to come into my life before starting to live? Had he and Tabby been waiting for me?

Reaching across the table, I took Alex's hand. "This is the right thing. I can feel it. This was *always* meant to be."

He nodded. "It really was. When things got so bad, I thought I'd never be happy again. I thought it would be Tabby and me alone for the rest of my life. Fortunately, I was wrong."

"Me, too," Tabby said, then slurped up a spaghetti noodle. "I love us."

I loved us, too. When I looked at the happiness in Alex's eyes, it was obvious he did as well. "We'll make a great family, Ky. You will be the matriarch of a very happy family."

Me, a matriarch?

At only twenty-two, I was on the cusp of becoming a mother of a three-year-old, the wife of a thirty-five-year-old, and had no idea what more would come my way.

And I never felt so ready for anything in my life.

23

ALEX

CLIMBING into our bed after Ky accepted my proposal, I never felt more connected. After our marriage, we'll feel even more of a union. "Hey there, fiancée," I said moving onto the bed next to her.

Opening her arms, she batted her brows at me. "Hey there, yourself, fiancée."

Our lips met and our bodies went flush against the other's as we slipped into the state we always did when we were alone: naked and unashamed. Life with Ky would be fantastic.

Pausing the kiss, I confided "Ky, I don't want to wait a long time to get married. Let's get the marriage license tomorrow and plan for the wedding right away. Our parents can help us this weekend. Hopefully, we can have something organized by the end of next month."

The smile that pulled her lips up on one side told me she liked that idea. "Carla will be my maid of honor. And my old roomies can be the bridesmaids. That means we'll need time to get the dresses done."

"Get going on that as soon as you'd like to." I kissed her again. "And I've got one more thing to get started on."

Looking into my eyes, she asked, "What's that?"

"Toss your birth control." I kissed her soft lips once more. "Ky, I want us to have a baby."

Her body shivered as she moaned, "Yes." Her lips pressed against my neck. "I would love to have your baby, Alex."

Moving my body over hers, I looked down at her. "I guess we should start practicing then."

She spread her legs, and I slipped right into her warm center. "I agree. Practice makes perfect, right?"

"Right." Being inside of her felt so right, and I knew it was the right time for us to start trying for a baby.

Ky had already proven herself to be a wonderful mother; I had no doubts she would make me even prouder with our own baby. She and I would make a family we could be proud of. We'll do it together—what a change that would be for me. I'd always done it mostly on my own.

Moving her body in a wavelike motion, Ky moaned as I moved inside of her. "Alex, this doesn't feel like reality. This has to be a dream; I'll wake up from it and find myself alone and miserable instead of happy and fulfilled."

"Shh," I whispered, then kissed her sweet lips. "This isn't a dream and nothing is going to wake you up from it." One would think it would be me who thought that. But I had faith we would get a hell of a lot more time than I had with Rachelle.

God couldn't possibly take two loves away from me in less than a decade.

As her hands moved over my back, Ky's foot ran up the back of my leg. I looked at her pretty face, letting each feature penetrate my mind and lodge into my memory. She smiled as I moved deeper into her. "Oh, yeah. How do you manage that, Alex?"

"A trade secret." I kissed her again, wanting to taste her.

As we made love, I wondered what our baby would look like. Tabby looked like her mother, so would our future kids look like Ky?

I wanted to see some of me in our future kids, too. Not that I didn't like the way Tabby looked. I knew she was meant to look like her mother. That way there would always be someone here to help me remember Rachelle.

Love was something I'd never completely understood—and now was no different. There was the love between a kid and their parents. Love between siblings. Love between a man and a woman and the love between parents and their children.

But how unlike the love between a man and a woman could be from one partner to another! The way I loved Ky and Rachelle was completely dissimilar.

Rachelle was refined, classy, and self-assured. Plus, Rachelle could be quite a bitch when things didn't go her way. I chalked that up to her wealthy upbringing.

And Ky was down to earth, sweet, and not at all self-assured. I loved all that stuff about her. And in a way, I loved her more than I ever loved Rachelle. Was it because Ky loved Tabby when she didn't have to? But I loved Ky more, and that was a fact.

Our bodies just fit like hand and glove. Her tits brushed just underneath me. Her hips pushed below mine. And the way her lips formed to mine seemed as if cut precisely to fit them. Everything about her body fit mine, but that wasn't all I loved about Ky.

Her nature was a thing I adored. Her lack of style made me smile. I loved picking out things for her to wear and getting her dolled up at the salon, too. I thoroughly enjoyed doing things for Ky.

Especially doing things that made her pant and scream like an animal. Grinding into her deep and steady, I felt her heart pounding against my chest. Sharp, freshly manicured nails dug into the flesh of my back.

Pulling back to look at her, I saw her glow begin as her body began its ascent into ecstasy. "Alex!" Her eyes flew open as her cunt clenched around my cock. "Oh, God!"

I moved faster and fucked her harder as her body clung to mine. As if she was pulling everything she could from me, Ky hung on, clamping down until I let go of what she needed. "Shit!" My cock jerked as I came inside of her, plunging in as deep as I could.

Sure, she wasn't off the birth control yet, but we were practicing, and I wanted to get it perfect for when the time did come. Ky was on oral birth control. After she stopped taking them, which would be the very next day, it would take approximately a month to get them entirely out of her system—a month for practicing religiously on making our baby.

When I caught my breath, I looked down at her as she perspired, beads of sweat falling down her temples. "How about that way? Think that might do the trick?"

Moving her hands up to my cheeks, she nodded. "Oh, yeah, that will be just fine. But let's not get lost in only one way, babe. There are many more ways you can get that sperm to bust through one of my eggs. No reason to limit ourselves."

Another thing Ky was that Rachelle wasn't. *Sexually adventurous.*

"I love you, Ky Rush. Soon to be Ky Arlen. My wife." I couldn't stop looking at her as tears sprang up in her pretty hazel eyes that turned very green all of a sudden. "I'm going to cherish every day with you. I won't take a single day for granted."

"How did I get so lucky, Alex?" She sniffled. "How did I, Ky Rush, get so lucky to have you love me?"

"I'm the lucky one," I whispered, then kissed her softly. "It's Tabby and me who got lucky when you came into our lives. They weren't miserable lives, but empty. The moment you came into our home, you brought something. And it grew until it filled this entire mansion with love."

A sob came out of her, and she put her hands over her face. "Stop it! You're killing me, Alex. It's sweet sentiment overload."

"Oh, yeah?" I chuckled as I kissed her face all over. "Better get used to hearing stuff like that because our wedding will be full of that kind of talk."

She whimpered as I kept up with the soft kisses. "No, you can't do that to me. You'll make me cry that whole day if you keep it up."

"Then you better get used to it, Ky." I rolled over, holding onto her, so we didn't part. Sitting her up on top of me, I took her tits into my hands. "I wonder how big these will get. And how juicy, too."

Rachelle didn't like me messing with her breasts, and I lusted after them during the pregnancy. I couldn't wait for Ky's to get all plump.

"Don't tell me you're one of those guys," Ky said as she rolled her eyes. "Ones who want to drink the milk."

"If you let me." I pulled her down and took one of her nipples between my lips, sucking gently, then let it go. "See, I can get you used to breastfeeding. That way your nipples won't hurt so much when the baby comes along. I'm only thinking of you, dear."

"Sure you are." She laughed and wiggled her tits in front of my face. "Keep doing that. I like it. It makes my tummy tickle on the inside."

Not one to leave a girl hanging, I took the other nipple between my lips and licked it, loving how it made her moan and drag her nails across my chest. There seemed to be nothing I did that Ky didn't like. And now I would have a lifetime of that.

A lifetime of being with the woman who made me smile with the simplest of gestures. A lifetime of being with a woman who loved my child. A lifetime of being with a woman I felt connected to so profoundly, I could feel it in my soul.

When I met Rachelle, I knew I loved her at first sight. But even with that kind of love, I never felt as if we were soul mates. Ky and I slipped into that kind of feeling. It hadn't always been there; we found it along the way somehow. I couldn't even pinpoint when that occurred.

"You're about to make me come, Alex," Ky panted as I sucked her delicious tit.

I wasn't about to stop. I wanted her to come all over my cock, knowing the contractions about to happen all around it would bring it pulsing back to life, and we'd have yet another session before falling asleep in an exhausted heap of spent flesh.

Her moans were like music to my ears as her body clenched around mine. I lifted her up and down, letting her tit go so she could stroke my now-erect cock with that pulsing pussy of hers. Looking into her eyes, I thanked God silently for sending her to me that fateful day. "You are my angel, Kyla Rush. My God-given angel. And I will always treat you as such."

She looked at me with teary eyes. "I hope this lasts, Alex. I hope this feeling of pure bliss lasts a very long time."

I do, too.

24

KY

"Why do I feel so nervous, Alex?" I whined as we waited for our parents to arrive for the weekend.

"I don't know, baby." He draped his arm over the back of the sofa we sat side by side on, letting his hand fall on my shoulder. "My parents are not like Tabby's other grandparents. My mom and dad are poles apart from them. And my younger brother is a cool guy. He'll be my best man. I bet he's going to flip."

"He wasn't your best man at your other wedding?" I bit my lower lip to stop it from quivering. I worried a lot about our wedding. I feared it would spark memories for Alex—memories he might not be aware of and dampen the day.

Shaking his head, he looked miffed. "No. I didn't pick the best man for that wedding. Claus put his cousin in that spot. And more of the Vanderhavens formed the rest of our wedding party. It wasn't a thing I got a say in since they paid for the whole thing. My parents and brother felt extremely out of place. They left five minutes into the reception."

"They won't feel out of place at our wedding. It will not be so fancy the love gets lost, you know what I'm saying?" I wasn't about to become one of those bridezillas on him. My family and friends, and Alex's, too, will feel at ease.

"I certainly do." He chuckled a little. "Would you like to see the wedding album? It's so—what would the best term be for it? Stoic." Alex nodded. "Yeah, that's it. Stoic. There are no smiles in the pictures. Smiles are considered silly when a Vanderhaven is being photographed."

How horrible. "I hope they're not that way with Tabby. I'd hate to think of her being unable to smile whenever she wants to."

"No, they're not." He kissed my cheek. "You think about her a lot, Ky. It's sweet." Moving one hand through my hair, he'd gone into a deep thought. "It's like you're her mom already." His blue eyes met mine. "After we get married, would you adopt Tabby? Become her real mother?"

What to say? It felt wrong to push her mother out of that role. "We'll see. She's young and may forget about her mother in time, and I honestly don't want that to happen."

"Adopting her won't mean we'll stop talking about Rachelle as her mother." Alex smiled then kissed my cheek again. "You're the most thoughtful and amazing woman I've ever met. It's an honor to be marrying you."

"The honor is all mine." I kissed him back. "So why should I adopt her then?"

"What if something happens to me?" he asked as he searched my eyes.

Eyes that had gone blurry with tears. "Don't say that." I wiped them away quickly. "I don't like to think about anything happening to you."

"I know." His arm moved around my shoulders to pull me closer to him. "But things happen. I'd like to know Tabby wouldn't be taken away by her grandparents. If you were her adopted mother, they couldn't."

"When you put it this way, of course. Right after we're married if you want to." I never wanted to lose Tabby. I'd do anything to prevent that from happening. "If I lost you and then her, too, it would devastate me." A shudder ran through me; then the doorbell ring. "They're here!"

Tabby dropped the blocks she'd been playing with to dart over to us. "Is that Gammy and Papa or Ky's mom and dad?"

Alex got up, pulling me up with him. "Let's go see." He scooped Tabby up with one arm and kept his other around me.

Heading to the foyer, I felt shaky. "I hope it's my parents."

Alex looked at me wide eyed. "Wow, I didn't think you had a selfish bone in your body, Ky."

"I have several." I smiled. "It would be nice to have my parents to back me on what a nice girl I am."

"You have me for that." He moved his arm off my shoulders to put it around my waist. "I'll always have your back, girl."

When we got to the foyer, I heard a voice similar to Alex's. "It's *your* family." I bit my lower lip staving off panic. Then I heard my mother's voice and my heart lifted with happiness. "Mom and Dad are here, too!"

Now I felt better—much better. As we came into the foyer, all eyes came to us. No one has been told about our impending nuptials. No one knew others would be there for the weekend, too. Not one of them said a word as they entered the lobby.

"Hey, you guys," Alex greeted them. "How convenient, you've all shown up at the same time. Let's get the introductions out of the way. "Ky, this is my mother, Naomi, Dad's name is Bruce, and that's my younger brother, Andrew. I'm the only one who gets to call him Andy."

I followed along, introducing my parents, "This is my mom, Susan, and my dad is David. Welcome to our weekend soirée, everyone."

Tabby tapped her dad on the shoulder. "I want to hug my gammy and papa!"

"Sure." Alex put her down, then went to shake my father's hand. "It's a pleasure to finally meet you, David."

Dad eyed me as he shook Alex's hand. "Pleasure to meet you, too, Alex. Tabby told us Ky works for you as the governess. So you can imagine my surprise at seeing your arm wrapped around her waist, right?"

Mom's eyes were glued to the ring on my left hand. Her hands flew to cover her mouth. Then I looked at Alex for what to do next. He was quick to educate them all, "Look, Ky and I have been seeing each other for a while now. None of you were aware. And there's more, too."

Tabby jumped up and down. "Can I tell them? Please!"

I nodded, and Alex agreed, "Okay, honey, tell them our great news."

Tabby's face glowed as she said, "We're getting married." She held her arms out as an enormous smile covered her face. "We're in love!" Hopping up and down, her dress billowed out with each jump.

Alex's mother came up to us, reaching out for my hand. "May I see the ring?"

Holding out my hand, she admired the ring. "Your son has great taste."

"He sure does." She looked back at her husband. "This rock makes my ring look like something out of a gumball machine, Bruce. You've got to see this."

Everyone took turns admiring the ring, but no words of congratulations. What I did hear was my father clearing his throat. "Ky, we'd like to have a word with you in private."

Looking at Alex, I gathered strength from him before taking my parents to another room to fill them in. With the door closed behind us in the library, I came clean, "I didn't tell you guys about Alex and me getting together because I didn't know what you'd say about it."

Dad's arms crossed over his chest. "He's a bit older than you, Ky."

I nodded. "Yes, he is. Thirteen years to be exact. But love knows no age difference, it seems."

"He's got a kid already, Ky," Mom added. "Are you ready to be that girl's mother?"

"Yes. I adore her, Mom. I love her so much. I don't know what I'd do without her." I held my arms out to them. "Can I have a hug and to hear the words I've been hoping to hear? I'm marrying a wonderful man. A doctor! A well-heeled one at that. And I love that man with everything in me."

Mom's eyes went to Dad's as she said, "She's never looked better, David. Maybe this is a good thing. She's always been an old soul."

Looking like he lost the battle, Dad conceded, "Congratulations, Ky. Am I walking you down the aisle?"

I hugged him. "Dad, I'd love nothing more than for you to walk me down the aisle. We're planning this weekend with all of you to have a wedding that will give us a lifetime of memories."

Mom started crying and got in on our hug, wrapping her arms around me from behind as I hugged Dad. "Oh, my baby girl is getting married!"

Should I tell them about our baby news? *Nah, I don't want to jinx it.* "So, let's give Alex congrats, too." Leading them to the living area, I heard them gasp as we entered the grand room.

Mom whispered, "This is so lovely."

Dad looked around. "So much leather."

"Yeah, Alex likes his leather furnishings alright." I led them over to where Alex and his family sat.

Before I could take a seat though, his mother and father stood as his father said, "Welcome to the family, Ky." His arms closed around me, and I immediately teared up.

"Thank you," I managed to choke out.

His mother took up where his father left off, taking me into her arms. "I'm going to have a daughter-in-law. This is so nice." She let me go, then looked me over. "Rachelle didn't have much to do with us. I hope you can make time to visit us, Ky. I'd love to have a better relationship with you."

"Mom," Alex's brother hissed. "Not cool."

Andrew was a few inches shorter than Alex but just about as hot. The girls at the wedding would be all over him. *I intend to make sure he'd be available for all that female attention.*

"So you're Alex's little bro, Andrew." I reached out to shake his hand, and he pulled me in for a hug instead.

"No way! You get over here and hug me." He laughed as he let me go. "Rachelle didn't have much use for me, either. I hope we can be close, Ky. I really do."

"Me, too." I liked them already. "So, are you single, Andrew?"

"At the moment I'm between girls." He smiled. "Why, you got a friend?"

Alex reached out from his seat on the couch and pulled me to sit on his lap. "There'll be more than a few bridesmaids who will turn your head, Andy. Since you're going to be my best man, you can have your pick."

The way his brother smiled... He was shocked. "You want *me* to be your best man? *Me?*"

Alex nodded. "Please say yes."

"Hell, yes!" His fist shot up in the air. "I'm going to throw you the best bachelor party in the history of raunchy parties."

"No strippers," I said quickly.

Nodding, Andrew agreed, "No strippers. Got it. Just some wild fun that he'll never forget. This is going to be so badass!"

I think so, too.

25

ALEX

We set a date for a month from that Saturday. Bella Luna Farms on the outskirts of town had a unanimous vote.

Securing a date at the chosen venue—only a month away—seemed daunting. Cherry, the event manager of Bella Luna, checked her computer, shaking her head as Saturday after Saturday was booked.

"No. There is no way in the world to get you in this coming month. The same date is available next year though." She smiled at me, pulling her glasses off, and then laying them on the desk. "How about that?"

Shaking my head, it wasn't the date we settled on. "See, I've already promised my fiancée we'd get married quickly. We're already trying for a baby. I don't want the baby to come before the marriage. Call me old-fashioned, but that's just the kind of man I am."

Cherry just shook her head. "That's respectable of you, Dr. Arlen, but all of our spaces are full."

"Our wedding party is only fifty people, Cherry." I thought of the grove of pines I passed on the way in. "What about the small grove of pine trees?"

"We don't provide wedding services there." She shook her head once more. "We have nothing for your guests to sit on. We call that area Squirrel Hill."

"I can pay you whatever you want for that area to accommodate our party. That would give you one more venue."

Tapping her fingernails on the desk, she contemplated my offer. "That would cost you, Doc."

"Give me a figure, Cherry. See if I blink." She had no clue about my financial status.

"Our fee isn't economic in the first place," she let me know. "When you add in building a whole venue, no matter how small, you're looking at upward of a hundred grand—give or take a few thousand dollars."

"Done." I pulled out one of my cards. "Put what you need to on my account."

Her eyes went wide, and she gasped. "Are you sure?"

"I do have one stipulation," Since I was paying to build a new venue, I should name it. "It's called Squirrel Hill, but can the venue itself be called something else?"

Taking my card, she ran it through to find it had no limit. "The sky's the limit." She looked at me. "What should this venue be called?"

"Fate on Squirrel Hill." I liked the sound of it, and I knew Ky would, too. "Fate is what brought my fiancée and I together. The name would suit many couples, don't you think?"

"Sure." With a shrug of her shoulders, she had no reason to deny me. "You'll have something beautiful for you and your fiancée, Dr. Arlen. Let me know what time you'd like the festivities to begin, and everything will be ready when your special day comes."

"I'll get back with you on that. Ky should pick the time."

I accomplished the primary goal of the day and knew Ky and the rest of my family wouldn't believe it.

"See you then, sir." Cherry couldn't stop smiling as she watched me leave her office.

She had every reason to smile. She just created a whole new

venue at no cost to them. Ky would love that we built and named it, too.

As I drove to the hospital to make my rounds, the rain started getting heavier. Seattle rain wasn't a thing we'd discussed. I hoped Cherry would make sure there would be adequate shelter in case of rain.

More details to hammer out, but we should get them all done in time. Nothing could bring me down, it seemed. I just couldn't get worried about a thing. All that really mattered was that Ky and I would be married in a month. Hopefully with a fetus inside of her, too.

The idea of having a baby with Ky took over my thoughts. Again, my mind traveled to how our first child would look. My hair, her eyes, or vice versa? A mixture of us would be good—at least on the first one.

When I'd run the number of children to add to our family by Ky, she frowned at me, saying we had to go with things as time went along. She didn't want to settle on any number. My number had been three, and she wasn't sure—too many or too few?

We had so much life to live; it seemed almost impossible. I missed out on too much with Rachelle. Now I'd get the chance again with Ky. A second chance to live a life full of love and happiness sounded like a gift from above.

As I pulled into the parking garage at the hospital, the entrance was blocked. A worker wearing an orange vest waved me to the side. Rolling down the window, I asked, "Are you guys almost done?"

"No." He pointed to the street. "You'll have to park on the street today. The parking garage will be open again tomorrow." He looked over his shoulder, then back at me. "I'm not supposed to say why it's closed, but let's just say there are more than a few celebrities in there."

"So, they're filming some movie?" I nodded. "Gotcha. I'll park elsewhere today."

As I drove off, I noticed all the cars parked along the street. Others were circling around to find a place to park.

With the rain getting lighter, I went ahead and drove a few blocks further. Parking was a-plenty, but the walk would take me a bit. As I got out of the car, my cell rang, and I pulled it out. "Hey, babe, how's it going?"

"You know how it's going, Alex," Ky said with a tense voice. "Did you get the place?"

"Well, kind of," I teased her.

"Kind of?" she worried. "What does that mean?"

"I didn't get the venue we talked about. The duck pond is out, and so is the grape house." I smiled, knowing she was most likely chewing on one of her nails.

"Maybe we can change the date," she said. "Make it later in the year. A month's time is short notice. I told you we'll have a hard time getting anywhere good."

"You have so little faith in me, Ky." I looked both ways, then crossed the nearly empty street.

"What does that mean?" she whined. "Are you screwing with me, Alex?"

Indeed. "What if we get married in a place that no one ever has?"

"That sounds kind of good, but kind of bad, too."

"We'll be the first couple to marry in that exact place." Will she think that was pretty special, the way I did?

"Where is this place?" she asked.

"Bella Luna Farms." I stopped at the next intersection as traffic picked up closer to the hospital.

"You just said we couldn't get it," she moaned. "Stop playing with me, Alex. Just tell me where."

"We *are* getting married at the place we wanted to." A car rushed passed me, making me take a step back. "Damn, this traffic is a nightmare."

Ky wasn't letting up. "We *are* getting married there? But *where* there?"

"There's this little, wooded area I'm getting a venue set up in. We'll be the first couple to get married right in that spot." I hoped she liked the name I'd picked out. "I named it Fate on Squirrel Hill."

"Hmm," she mulled it over. "That's kind of cool."

More cars sped by, and I looked down the street to see if there was anywhere I could cross the busy street that had a stoplight at it but saw nothing. "I think fate brought us together; that's how I came up with it."

"Aww, that's so sweet, babe. What are you doing now?" she asked.

"Trying my best to get to the hospital, but this traffic is horrible." I looked up the street to find a safe place to cross and saw some people waiting on the sidewalk. There must be a traffic light there, and I headed in that direction.

"Traffic?" Ky asked. "You always use the parking garage. What traffic?"

"It's closed." I sped up a bit as people were moving and figured the light must've changed as the cars stopped, too. "Apparently, they're filming in there right now."

"Oh, yeah?" she squealed. "Johnny Depp's in town. I heard that on the news this morning. How cool!"

"Johnny Depp, huh?" I caught up to where the people had crossed and saw the sign was still showing, telling me I could cross. "That *is* cool. I'll see you later, baby. Kiss my little princess for me. I love you, bye."

"I love you too. Bye, my sexy man."

Ending the call, I put the cell in my pocket, then heard the sound of an engine revving. Picking up my already fast pace, I still had half the street to go before getting safely to the other side. "Shit! I hate crossing streets." I got uneasy anytime I had to cross streets. And to be left in the middle of one with so many cars on either side had my anxiety heightened.

Just as my foot touched the curb, the sound of that same engine revved up again. When I turned to look, I saw only yellow before it all went black.

26

KY

Pulling up the website for Bella Luna Farms, Tabby and I looked at the map on the screen to see where her daddy set things up for us. "Oh, right here, Tabby." I pointed to where the trees were and saw they called it Squirrel Hill. "This is where your daddy and I will get married."

"In the trees?" she asked as she looked at me questioningly. "Where squirrels live?" She shook her head. "Nope. I don't like it."

Trying to convince a three-year-old her daddy had excellent taste, I said, "Daddy said they'll build something that we can get married in. I'm sure it'll be something wonderful."

Her tiny forehead wrinkled as she squinted her eyes and seemed to be deep in thought. Finally, she nodded. "Yes."

Her arms wrapped around me, then her lips pressed against my cheek. "I want to call you Mommy, Ky."

The way my heart skipped a beat and a smile curved my lips told me I loved this little girl. "Oh, Tabby, I can't wait to hear you call me that. It's like a dream come true. I'm about to have my own family. And one day your daddy and I will have you some baby brothers and sisters of your very own, too."

"Baby sister, yes." Her nose wrinkled. "Baby brothers," she shook her head. "No."

Pulling her onto my lap, I spun around in the office chair in Alex's home office. "Aw, come on, baby boys can be nice, too."

"Uh, uh," she protested. "Baby girls are nicer."

I'll have to do my best to give this kid a baby sister. Either give her a baby sister or make Tabby think she really wanted a baby brother.

"When the time comes, I'm sure you'll be happy with whatever we have." I bounced her on my knee. "Right?"

She laughed as her head shook once more. "No."

Oh, hell.

Deciding to change the subject, I went turned back to the computer. "Help me pick out a flower girl dress for you!"

"Yes!" Her green eyes sparkled with delight. "One with flowers. And ribbons in my hair. Nice shoes, too. And…"

I stopped her with the page I opened. "Like any of these dresses?"

Nodding, her eyes glued to the monitor, her little finger ran over each dress. "So many beautiful dresses. I like all of them!"

"How about one that matches mine?" I asked clicking to the next page. "That way we can both look like brides."

"I like that." We found the dress at the same time. "That one."

"I agree." I clicked it, got one in her size, then clicked the Order button. "The dress is on its way. Now the shoes."

The way she looked at me with arched browns nearly made me laugh as she asked, "Can I wear high heels?"

Kissing the tip of her cute little nose "No way, little lady. Only flats for you. They'll be very pretty and comfortable. You'll have to wear them all day. You won't want them to be uncomfortable." I smiled. "I'm wearing flats, too. I don't care what Carla says about wearing heels on your wedding day."

Tabby nodded. "Yeah, we like to be comfortable."

Already she followed my fashion lead. "Comfort over beauty" had become my motto since working with Carla concerning the bridal fashions. "If one searches hard enough, one can find beauty and comfort in one."

Tabby nodded. "Yeah. We like comfort."

I found shoes that had small red roses on the toes. "Oh, Tabby! Look at these."

The way her face lit up made my heart skip a beat. "They're so pretty! Can I have them? Please!"

"They'll look adorable with the dress." I clicked the button and made the purchase. "Shopping with you is easy, Tabby."

"And fun," she said, nodding. "When's Daddy coming home? I want to show him my dress."

We should do something sweet to include her even more than just as a flower girl. How can we include her in the ceremony? Tabby should feel a part of us. All us should feel like a real family.

Taking a second, I looked up to give a silent prayer, thanking God and anyone else up there who might've had something to do with the love we had.

Tabby put her hands on either side of my face, "Ky, when's Daddy coming home?"

Blinking at her, I came out of my prayer. "I'm not sure. He has rounds to make. He'll be here in time to see your dress and shoes before you go to bed. Don't worry about that." I got up, carrying her with me. "What do you say we get a healthy snack and read a book while we eat it?"

"Grapes." She smiled at me as she took a lock of my hair, twirling it around her finger. "And tropical punch, too!"

"Sounds good to me." I had a craving for peanut butter and bananas that had come out of nowhere. "I'll see if Rudy will make me something, too. This craving just snuck up on me."

"What's a craving?" Tabby asked as I pushed open the kitchen door.

Rudy heard her. "A craving is when a person really really wants a particular food. And who's craving what?"

I raised my hand as I sat Tabby on a barstool at the island in the middle of the kitchen. "It's me. It's peanut butter with slices of bananas."

"On bread?" he asked as he headed to the pantry to get the things.

"No. Just a spoonful of peanut butter and one sliced banana. That'll be good."

Tabby piped up, "I want grapes, please. And tropical punch, too, Mr. Rudy."

"You're in for a treat," he said. "I've made fresh tropical punch this morning. A pineapple, two oranges, a mango, a peach, and strawberries. This might be my best tropical punch ever."

It sounded like that, too. "Yummy. I can't wait to try it." Running my hand through Tabby's blonde hair, I let her know how lucky she was to have such a great chef taking care of our nutrition, "We're lucky to have what we have, Tabby."

Looking confused, she asked, "What do we have?"

"Chef Rudy." I looked over and gave him a smile. "He makes sure we get lots of healthy things to eat and drink. And they all taste great, too."

"Yes," Tabby said as she nodded. "And they're pretty, too." She pointed to the way he was cutting the banana. "Banana roses, Ky."

"Rudy, you don't have to go to all that trouble." He didn't have to make me a five-star snack.

"It's no trouble at all." He proved that as he finished making our snacks in record time. "See?"

"What can't you do?" I asked him in amazement.

"Lots of things." He put the plates in front of us. "Like mowing the lawn or cleaning gutters. But in the kitchen, I am a star!"

"You are a star!" Tabby agreed. "Thank you, Mr. Rudy."

"You are most welcome, Miss Tabby." He looked at me as I used a tiny fork to eat my snack with. "And how do you like that, Miss Ky?"

"I'm missing something. I can't put my finger on it, but it needs more." It just wasn't hitting the spot for me.

But Rudy did. He went to the pantry and came out with a jar of honey. "Allow me to drizzle some of this on top. I do believe you will find what's been missing."

One bite told me he was right. "Yes. Oh, yeah. This is what I wanted. You're a mind reader."

"I just know what foods pair well." He put our glasses of punch in front of us. "Enjoy your snacks, ladies. I need to go to the market for tonight's dinner. Beef Wellington is the main course."

I'd heard of that, but had no idea what it really was. "Rudy, what's in Beef Wellington?"

"Filet mignon and I make a pâté of grilled red onions and portabella mushrooms," he explained. "It's wrapped up in a crescent roll-type of dough."

Tabby's eyes went wide. "Like a pie with meat?"

"Sort of." He shrugged. "It's a bit fancier than a meat pie, though."

"It sounds delicious," I said as my stomach grumbled, and I put my hand over it as my cheeks heated with embarrassment. "Oh! Seems my tummy thinks so, too."

He left us alone, chuckling all the way out. Then the house phone rang, and my heart stopped. Only the Vanderhavens called on that line—at least since I lived here anyway.

I tried not to look nervous as we ate our snacks. Chloe would answer the call; she always did. My other fingers were crossed, and I offered a prayer that it would be a sales call.

When Chloe's voice drifted into the kitchen, "Ky?" a knot formed in my stomach.

"Darn it." I got up, and Tabby looked at me with confusion. "I've got to take this call, Tabby. Can Chloe sit with you for a moment?"

"Okay." Tabby went on, eating her grapes that Rudy cut in halves.

Chloe met me at the door. "Ky, it's for you. I'll watch after Tabby while you take the call."

"Please," I said, then looked out the door. "Where is the phone?"

She handed me the cordless phone out of her apron pocket. "You can use the other room if you'd like."

Expecting Tabby's grandparents on the other end of the line, I nodded. "Good idea." Walking out, after closing the door, I said, "Ky here."

"Ky, this is Dr. Reagan Dawson at Saint Christopher's. Is someone there to watch Alex's daughter?"

"The housekeeper is here." I felt odd and sat on the nearest chair. "Is everything okay?"

"No," came her soft reply. "Alex was in an accident."

I stopped breathing. "No."

She went on, "I'm afraid so. You should come down here to the Emergency Room. They'll bring you to us."

"Is he..." a lump formed in my throat.

"Tell the driver to bring you down here. Don't drive yourself," she recommended. "You'll hear everything when you get down here."

Numbness washed over me. "OK."

Please don't die, Alex!

27

ALEX

A FLASH of white light and the sound of electricity shooting through the air made me sit up and look at the sky. People all around me were whispering. Not being able to make anything out of what was said, I focused on the light that only became brighter and brighter.

"Alex," came the soft sound of a woman's voice.

A voice I recognized. "Rachelle?"

Squinting, I couldn't see anything but light. "Alex, you're doing a great job with our daughter."

"Thanks, Rachelle." I put my hand above my eyes to try to shield some of the light to catch a glimpse of my deceased wife. And then it hit me. *Rachelle is dead!*

"I don't like to call it being dead, Alex."

Am I dead, too?

"No, you're not. Not by a long shot." The light moved in slow waves as she went on, "You're a doctor, Alex. What do you think happens after one is hit by a car?"

"I was hit by a car?" I looked around, then felt myself floating upwards, and when I looked down, I saw it all. My body lay on the sidewalk and people circled around me. "Blood is pooling behind my head. Not much, though." The hospital was close. "They need to get me over there. Harris can patch me up."

Rachelle's voice came near my ear. I could feel her breath move over it as she said, "You're not breathing, Alex. Try to breathe. That's essential, you know."

A woman said, "He's not breathing. Does anyone know CPR?"

"I do," a man called out. "Let me through."

"Sounds like the guy from Pirates of the Caribbean," I said.

Dressed all in black with his dark hair slicked back with shiny gel, a man moved through the crowd to get to me. "Everyone back. Give me room to work."

"Hey, it's the guy from the movie!" I laughed as the famous actor gave me CPR. Then I wasn't floating anymore. I was on the hard ground, the light was gone, and raindrops were falling on my face. And there loomed the man who'd saved me. "Hey, Johnny Depp."

He looked around, stunned. "Oh, no. I'm not him. I'm his stunt double." He got up and looked at me. "Are you okay, Mister?"

"Not really." Everything hurt enormously. "But I am breathing. Thanks."

"Good luck then." He disappeared into the crowd. Their eyes followed the man and murmurs of disbelief were heard above the wailing sirens.

Trying not to move my head, I tried moving my fingers and failed to do so on the right hand. *Shit!*

Paramedics walked through the crowd, dispersing it as they came through. "Out of the way, people. Go on. There's nothing to see here." They stopped as they saw me.

Dale's jaw gaped. "Dr. Arlen, it's you."

"Yeah," I said quietly as my strength was dwindling. "Get Harris up here. I can't move my fingers on the right hand." Things began to fade as they moved me to the gurney. "Pressure... on back of... head."

"We've got you, Doc," Dale told me as they put me into the back of the ambulance. "Take it easy. I'll make sure Dr. Dawson is ready for you."

Being moved had really taken a toll on me, and I must've gone out for a while. When I woke back up, there were lights in my eyes.

Harris's eyes and other sets of eyes were on mine. "Hi, Alex," he said. "You cracked your skull."

"So you shaved my head. I'll look dimwitted in my wedding photos now."

"You'll look great. Only the back was shaved." He looked at the nurse who assisted him. "Watch his toes and tell me if the left big toe moves."

Being under the knife during brain surgery wasn't done under anesthesia. Well, not the kind that knocks you out anyway. Lucky for me, I didn't freak out when someone was doing surgery on me.

"It did, Doctor," the nurse said.

"I felt it move, but I didn't think about moving it," I told them. "And I'd like to add that my body feels nice and warm. Cozy. I believe I am thinking rationally. There's slight pressure in the area of my cerebellum. But I'm not exhibiting signs of damage."

Harris asked, "What colors can you see, Alex?"

"Mostly white. It's so bright in here. The colors are dim in comparison to the lights." I stopped as I knew instinctively what area of my brain had been damaged. "Ah. The occipital lobe is where the problem is."

"Precisely," Harris confirmed. "That is where the fracture is. And your right fingers aren't moving because of pressure on the cerebellum caused by the dent on your skull. I'm fixing that."

"That explains the white light and me thinking I was looming over my body back there." But that didn't explain the sound of Rachelle's voice. "You sure there's no other damage, Harris? The temporal lobe might have some, too. I heard my lifeless wife talking to me. If there's damage there, too, then I can explain all that's happened to me."

"Sorry, Alex. There's no other injury." He chuckled. "Maybe you've turned into a psychic. Did she tell you the future?"

"No." He was kidding. "It was most likely my subconscious telling me things I wanted to hear. It seemed so real, though. I get it now when people have told me what they've seen and heard. It does seem like it's really happening."

"The brain is a tricky thing." Harris directed the nurse, "Pick up his right hand and let's see if his fingers move, then if he can move them himself."

She looked at me with her brows raised. "They're moving. Dr. Arlen?"

It took a lot of focus but they move. "I did it!"

"Yes, you did," she said.

Harris sounded pleased. "Great. It would be best if I kept you in a medically induced coma for three days to let this heal. Do you concur, Dr. Arlen?"

"I would do the same thing." But I wanted to talk to Ky. "Hey. This is unorthodox, but do you know if Ky is here?"

Someone in the gallery spoke up, and my eyes went to where the voice came from. "I'll get her," it was Reagan. "She's just outside."

Harris gave the order, "Drape him back here, so we don't terrify her."

"She doesn't need to see me looking like a bloody science experiment." She'd already been pretty shaken up. "I just want her to know I love her, and I'm not going anywhere." *I just wish I could really see her.*

Her pretty hazel eyes, her ash-blonde hair, her pink lips, and cheeks. Instead, all I'd see would be blurry white. But I'd get to see her, and that was better than nothing.

"Alex?" Ky asked. "You're awake?"

My eyes traveled to where her voice come from. The distance proved too great to see anything more than a wavy white shadow. "Ky! Yeah, I'm awake. For now, anyway. My occipital lobe was damaged. That means I can't see well. It typically takes three to five days for that to be nursed back to health. And the first three days should be spent with uninterrupted rest to speed the healing process. So, I'm going to be asleep for a few days. But I'm not about to expire on you, baby."

"Thank God," I heard her say with tear-laced words. "Alex, I love you."

"I love you, too, baby. It'll be alright. You'll see." I tried to see her so bad it made the back of my head hurt. "Okay, take me out, Harris." I held my hand up and moved my fingers in with a small wave. "See you in three days, my love. Kiss Tabby for me and tell her Daddy loves her."

Sobbing was all I heard before Reagan walked Ky out of the gallery. Harris offered me a few words of encouragement, "She'll be okay. Reagan and I will look after them, Alex. You just rest and get better. I'm looking forward to that wedding next month."

And then I heard nothing else.

The blips of a cardiac monitor were the first thing I heard when I started to wake back up. I liked the steady pulse my heart was making. Nothing hurt, so that was a plus. The meds hadn't worn off enough to open my eyes or even speak. But I could hear and that was the start of my waking up. When feminine voices came into the room. One of them was Ky's as she said quietly, "I just miss her so much, Susan. I wish they hadn't insisted on taking Tabby back to Spokane with them."

My mother was with her. "Rachelle's parents have always intimidated me. If David hadn't had to go right back to Denver to the business, then he wouldn't have let them take her. But I just don't have that backbone with them that he and Alex do. Once Alex is better, our girl will be back where she belongs."

"He will. The house feels so empty without her or Alex. I hate it," Ky said. "I've been staying with my friends at my old apartment. I can't sleep alone in that big bed without him in it. And I can't be in the house without them in it, either."

She's left our home? And Tabby's been taken away?

The heart monitor sped up and then something in my chest cramped. Bright light filled my eyes again as everyone's voice became whispers. I heard Rachelle's voice again, "Alex, what are you doing?"

"They took Tabby! Why'd you let them take her? Ky's her mother now. You've got to make them stop. Make them stop!"

"He's having a cardiac episode," a woman said. "We have to keep him sedated. He's not ready to come out yet."

Slowly, the light faded and I heard Harris say, "Two more days."

My mother and Ky weeping were the last thing I heard.

Don't cry, please don't cry.

28

KY

CARLA STARED at me as I sat on the sofa, trying to stop crying. "Come on, Ky. He's going to be alright. They said there was no damage to his heart. They just tried to pull him out of the medically induced coma too soon."

"Yeah, but this scares me, Carla." She didn't understand what Alex's accident did to me. "I can see it all very clearly now. Alex could die. If not today, then one day. I *will* lose him one day, and that pain is unbearable."

"What the hell are you saying, Ky?" Carla asked me as she handed me more tissues.

I'd been doing little else than thinking about what losing Alex and Tabby would be like. I found an emptiness there I couldn't stand. "Loving them is leaving me with too much to lose. If I lose Alex, I lose Tabby, too. Not that I wouldn't be able to care for her the way she deserved, but I'd want to keep her with me if anything happened to him. And now that this has happened, her grandparents will do everything in their power, which is vast, to keep her away from me. Even adopting Tabby won't help. Claus mentioned that when I told him what Alex asked me to do, once we're legally married."

"Who cares what old moneybags says?" she asked, blissfully unaware of reality.

"The courts, for one." I blew my nose and tried to stop myself from crying. "My head hurts, my chest hurts, and my nose hurts from blowing it so much. All this and I have a lot of faith that Alex will wake up and be okay again. What will happen if he actually dies, Carla?"

I might die right along with him. There was this idea in my head that I'd lie down on his grave and just not get up until I was with him again.

What kind of life would that be?

"You *will* go on if he dies," Carla said. "Haven't you learned anything from Alex? He lost his wife and the mother of their young daughter. He had to raise the baby all alone, Ky. He stayed strong for her. And you will have her, too, if anything should happen. You'll have her and any other kids you two have. Don't spazz out now. Not when you've had this great influence all this time. Learn from Alex's example. You *can* go on after the person you love dies."

How did Alex do it? For Tabby was all I could suppose. I couldn't have Tabby anymore if Alex didn't make it. The Vanderhavens would pull Tabby away from me if I had her half-brothers and sisters, too.

"There's so much I hadn't thought about, Carla." I wiped my eyes with a fresh tissue. "There is more to lose by marrying Alex than there is to gain."

"That's just insane," she got up and threw her hands in the air. "That man is smart, sweet, and from what you've told me, fantastic in the sack. Let's add in the fact he adores you, gives you more than you ever asked for, and have you ever seen a man that hot before?" She shook her head to emphasize her point. "No. You. Have. Not."

"But the hold he has on my heart is scary." I blew my nose, then winced with pain since it had become chapped. "And Tabby has the same hold. I'm lost without them, Carla. A few months ago I didn't even know them, and now they've got their claws all up in my heart, and I think even in my soul. If Alex dies, not only will his claws rip my heart to shreds, Tabby's will, too, when I no longer have her in my life, either. It's a lose-lose issue. Can't you see that?"

"Ky, every time you take a step, do you know the chances of you tripping and falling are like eighty percent?"

She was trying to help, but now she was just coming up with the most random shit. "You're making that up. You can't possibly know the percentage for that. And sure, when you walk, you might fall, okay. Skinned-up knees don't hurt like this does. This," I pounded my chest, "this is worse than a knife being plunged into your heart a thousand times. I can't believe the pain, and I am not even dying. How bad must a heart attack must hurt if this isn't killing me?"

She had no idea how much everything hurt me. My stomach ached all the time. My chest hurt more than anything else, but even my arms and legs ached. It didn't seem possible for my emotions to have this much effect on my body. But it was all very authentic.

"Maybe, ask one of those doctors at the hospital to help you out, Ky?" Carla cocked one brow at me. "Get something to calm your ass down?"

"Pills?" I asked her with disgust.

"Yes, pills, Ky." Her eyes rolled. "People need help sometimes. It's not like you're going to pop Xanax all the time. You just need to calm down right now. You're saying your chest hurts. What if something is really going on? Get it checked out. Having a heart attack at twenty-two isn't out of the realm of possibility."

Clutching my chest, I wondered if she's right. "Reagan is a cardiologist. Maybe she could see me."

Sitting perfectly still, I tried to listen to my heart. Am I making myself sick on purpose. Would I actually die if Alex did?

"You should totes ask for her help, Ky." Carla got up and went to the kitchen, coming back with a glass of wine. "Drink this for now. You need to chill out."

I took the glass from her and took a drink. "I've got so much to think about. Love might be too much for me. At least right now, it might. Alex and I have moved too fast. I can see that now. What it would do to me for anything to happen to him or Tabby? I'm too young. I can't deal—you know?"

Carla's dark brows furrowed. "You know, Ky, I wouldn't be a worthy maid of honor if I let you take the coward's way out of the marriage. I've known you almost our whole life. You love this man. You love his little girl. I don't think you will ever love anyone as much as you love those two."

She was right. "And that's why I've got to end it. It's too much. I can't take it."

"End it?" Alarm filled her face. "What would it do to that man? What would that little girl do if she never saw you again?"

"Maybe they're both tougher than I am." How had they got through losing Rachelle? Because they had each other. I would be alone if I ever lost Alex. How my best friend couldn't understand that floored me. "And who's side are you on anyway? I'm the one you should be worrying about, Carla. I am your best friend. You haven't even gotten to really know Alex or Tabby."

"It doesn't matter I haven't known them long," she said as she sat down next to me, draping her arm around my shoulders. "I've seen their effect on you, Ky. You've blossomed. You've grown in ways no one our age could have so quickly. I am on your side, girl. You should know that. What kind of a friend would let you throw this away because of what it will feel like if you lose them?"

"Chances are pretty high Alex will die before me," I reminded her. "He *is* thirteen years older."

"And chances are both of you will be old and gray with grown children by that time." She ran her hand through my hair, pushing it off my face. "Why don't you call the grandparents and ask if you can say hello to Tabby? It would make her feel better to hear from you. It will make you feel better to hear her voice, too."

Pulling out my cell, I looked at it for a long time. "You might be right." Getting up, I went outside to make the call. The night air, crisp and clean, cleared my head as I swiped her grandparents' last name.

"Hello, Vanderhaven residence. Bartholomew speaking. How can I help you this evening?"

"Bartholomew, this is Ky. I'd like to speak with Tabitha." I crossed my fingers he'd let me. It wouldn't surprise me if they'd already written Alex off and thought I didn't need to interact with their granddaughter.

Tabby's voice in the background made my heart spring, and a smile took over. "Is that Ky? Is that Ky?"

How did she know it was me? I loved that she did. "Please, sir. Please let me speak to her."

He didn't say a word. The next thing I heard was Tabby asking, "Is this Ky?"

A knot had formed in my throat, and I had to clear it before I could say, "It's me, my sweet little princess."

"I've missed you!" she shouted. "How's Daddy?"

"Still sleeping." I didn't want her to know about the incident when they tried to wake him. "It'll be a couple more days before he wakes up."

"Ky, can you come get me?" she asked innocently. "I want to see when Daddy wakes up. If I'm there, he'll get better fast."

"Let's see if we can do that, Tabby. Is one of your grandparents around?" I squared my shoulders, ready for a fight. For Tabby's sake. She was right; her daddy would get better faster with us both by his side.

"I'm here with Barthy," she let me know.

That pissed me off. The reason they took her was because they were upset I left her with Chloe when I came to the hospital that first day. "I'll tell you what, Tabby. Steven can drive me up there, and I *will* pick you up. You're coming home, sweetie."

This being pushed around shit is over. That girl needs me to stand up and fight for what's right.

After ending the call, I called Steven to come get me; we were going to Spokane and coming back with Tabby.

When I came back inside, Carla was looking at me with wide eyes. "You look different. There's fire in your eyes. What's up?"

"You're right. With great love comes great pain. But that's okay. It's the way it's meant to be." I walked over and drained the wine glass I'd only taken a sip of. "I'm done being steamrolled by Tabby's grandparents. I've got this rock on my finger. I *am* Alex's fiancée, not just a girlfriend. No judge in the world would say I don't have the right to make sure his little girl is at his side when he wakes up."

"Whoa." Carla had been rendered speechless. Almost. "I had no idea I could motivate anyone as quickly. You really have chosen the right maid of honor."

"I do select well, don't I?" I tapped my temple. "So why would I make the wrong choice with who I love?"

"You haven't made wrong choices there." Carla got up to walk with me to the door as a knock came to it. It was the driver. "I'll be here if you need me. Go get your little girl, Ky. Take her to her daddy and get your family in order."

And that's just what I aim to do.

29

ALEX

Lying in bed, so dark I couldn't see a thing, the sound of breathing came from beside me. As my eyes adjusted to the darkness, I found myself back in my home in Spokane, Rachelle by my side. Her soft blonde hair splayed out over the white pillowcase her pretty head rested on.

"Rachelle?" I reached out to touch her then her body disappeared. Emptiness took her place—a vast hole that left me feeling sick and alone.

"Alex," came another soft voice. "Come on, Alex, wake up."

Ky.

Looking at the empty spot on the bed, I knew I wasn't supposed to stay there any longer. My life wasn't over—not by a long shot.

"Bye, Alex," came Rachelle's voice. "You're doing all the right things. Go live your life and love like you might never see tomorrow. I wish I would've lived my life that way. I did love you, Alex. Even though I rarely said the words."

"I know you did," I whispered. "I loved you, too. I didn't say the words a lot, either. But I've learned from that. I let Tabby know I love her every day. I'll never stop."

"Alex, come on, Babe. It's me, Ky. I love you. I want to see those beautiful blue eyes of yours. Open them up for us."

"Please, Daddy."

Tabby's here?

Although not easy, my will had me opening my eyes. And there were my two girls, with smiles on their faces and tears in Ky's eyes. "Hi," I croaked out with a hoarse voice. Not using it in a few days made it sound odd and unfamiliar.

Tabby looked stunned. "Daddy, are you okay? What happened to your voice?"

Harris put his hand on my daughter's shoulder. "He hasn't spoken in five days, Tabby. It'll take time for his vocal cords to get back into shape. He'll be talking like your daddy before you know it."

Ky wouldn't let go of my hand, and I felt the pressure. "Missed you," I whispered. It felt better to whisper than to speak normally.

"Missed you more." She pulled my hand up to kiss it. "I'm so pleased you're awake."

Looking at Tabby, I remembered talk that her grandparents had her. If that memory was correct, then how did Ky manage to get her back?

So many questions, but my voice just wasn't up to it yet. "Jell-O."

Harris nodded. "I'll get that. Some warm broth will help, too. Not to worry, Alex." Looking at Ky, he took the hint. "Hey, Tabby, do you want to come with me to get your dad something to soothe his throat?"

"Yes." Tabby took Harris's hand, and he led her out of the room, leaving Ky and me alone.

Ky leaned over, kissing my forehead. "You scared me. Try not to do that."

I nodded. Seeing her with my recovered senses made my heart swell. "I'll try. You're so beautiful. I love you so much."

Wiping her eyes with the back of her hand, she sniffled. "This will be the last of the tears, Alex. Now that you're awake and on the road to recovery, I've made a vow to stop all the crying. You've made it through the hardest part; you'll make it home for certain."

I remembered her saying she left our home.

"You heard that?" She looked peculiar. "You knew I left?"

I nodded. "I'm glad you came back. That's *your* home, Ky."

"It didn't feel like it without you or Tabby in it." She gripped my hand. "By the way, we never have to lose sleep about the Vanderhavens taking Tabby away if anything happens to you. I straightened them out."

I couldn't believe it. "You did what?"

She smiled. "They took Tabby when they came to see you here. The fact I left Tabby with Chloe to come here made them angry, and they took her back to Spokane, telling me they will not bring her home until you were there, too. And they went so far as to say if you didn't come home, neither would she."

I hated that Ky and Tabby had gone through that. "I'll fix that."

She shook her head. "You don't have to. When I talked to Tabby on the phone, they were going about their lives as usual, and Tabby was with their butler. So Steven took me there, and I got our kid."

She called Tabby *ours*. "I love you so much."

"I love you, too. And I love Tabby, too. I'm her mother. I don't care if we aren't officially married yet. I don't care if she's not yet legally adopted. She is mine. I love her with all of my heart. I'm her mother in almost every sense of the word. I wasn't about to leave her there. She needed to be with you as much as I did."

"I needed her, too. Her voice is what made me open my eyes. Thank you." Ky had taken on the Vanderhavens and won.

"It wasn't that much of a fight." Ky ran her hand over my cheek. "When I approached them with reasonable words that I wasn't just their granddaughter's babysitter, I was her mother in all the ways that mattered. And seeing the way Tabby clung to me—they knew I wasn't lying. They were finally convinced."

"You're amazing." At times, even I had a tough time standing up to them. Pulling her to me, I wrapped my arms around her. "Thank you for coming into our lives. Thank you for being you, Ky."

"Stop it." She kissed my cheek before pulling herself out of my arms to wipe more tears out of her eyes. "You're making me cry again. I'm breaking my vow."

Looking at her, I made the right decision by asking her to marry me. No one could be more perfect for Tabby and me. Reaching out, I put my hand on her flat stomach. "Have you checked to see if you're pregnant yet?"

She shook her head. "Not without you, Alex. I wouldn't do that without you being there."

My eyes went to the bathroom. "Do it now."

"I'll have to buy a test." She looked at me with glistening eyes. "I am a few days late. That might just be due to stress, though."

"It might." I nodded. "But it might not." I wanted to know if she was pregnant. My patience wasn't functioning the way it normally did. "Please get a test, then come back. I have to know one way or the other."

"I'll leave once they get back." She looked over her shoulder. "What about Tabby?"

"She's fine here with me. The nurses around can help out. Don't wait. Go now." What was wrong with me? But I couldn't stop thinking about the baby.

With a kiss goodbye, Ky left and I watched her go, knowing our love would stand the test of time. Rachelle was gone. No one could ever bring her back. She hadn't really visited me. It was all in my injured brain. But it felt good to think so, and that she'd told me to love like there'd be no tomorrow.

Maybe that was why I lacked patience. I didn't know if tomorrow would come and wanted to experience everything as soon as I could.

Harris and Tabby came back, and Tabby asked, "Where's Ky?"

"I sent her on an errand," I told her.

Harris pulled the table over to me, putting the Jell-O on it. "Do you think you can feed yourself?"

I moved my arm up to rest it on the table, but it took a lot. "Man, this is difficult."

Tabby hopped up on the bed and took the spoon. "I'll feed you, Daddy. Don't worry."

Tears were burning the backs of my eyes, and the sentiment

wasn't lost on Harris either as he used his fingers to hold back tears that had sprung in his eyes. "Oh, hell." He shook his head. "I'll leave you two alone. Push the button if you need anything."

"Open wide, Daddy," Tabby said as she scooped the green stuff out of the container. "It's good for you."

I took the bite, trying not to cry with each spoonful she gave me. But it wasn't easy. And when a tear slipped out, I saw the odd look in her eyes. "Daddy's just happy to see you, Tabby."

She shrugged. "Oh, okay. I missed you so much." She put another bite into my mouth. "Ky got me. I was so happy. Ky told me you were sleeping."

Ky came back into the room, a small brown bag in her hand. She held it up. "Got it." Her eyes moved over Tabby and I. "Helping Daddy eat, Tabby?"

"Yes. His hands aren't working" She smiled. "I'm a big helper."

"Yes, you are." Ky looked at me with a huge smile. "Here it goes then. Soon we'll know if we've done the job or have to get back at."

I nodded as Tabby gave me another bite.

In a few minutes, we'll know if I'm going to be a daddy again.

30

KY

THE WEATHER PERFECT, the sky a brilliant blue that shone above the tall pine trees, and the smell of roses made all my senses blissful as I stood with my father at the end of the green carpet leading me to my man.

Alex looked handsome as he stood there, waiting for me. But first Tabby tossed red rose petals that matched the red roses on her shoes. Walking slowly, the way we'd practiced, Tabby didn't rush as she took the rose petals a handful at a time.

When she got to her daddy, she handed my maid of honor, Carla, the little basket she carried. "Here, Carla." Then she held her arms up for her father to pick her up. "Here I am, Daddy."

Our guests laughed quietly as Alex picked his daughter up. "Are you ready for Ky to come join our family, Tabby?"

She nodded, and tears welled up behind my eyes as she said, "I am ready."

With a nod from Alex, the wedding march started playing through the speakers, and my father took me down the aisle as I tried not to cry out loud. Tears trickled down my cheeks as I went to join Alex's family.

My father whispered, "You're going to be very happy, Ky." He kissed my cheek through the veil that covered my face and then let me go before taking his seat next to my mother.

"I know." I handed the bouquet of red roses to Carla who smiled at me. "Thank you."

She nodded. "You're welcome."

No one knew how I'd panicked when Alex was in the hospital. Carla kept that a secret. I didn't want Alex to learn how frightened I was and that I even entertained the thought of not going through with the marriage.

Turning to look at my family, I had to reach out for Alex's hand as my knees went weak. He took it, holding it and looking at me. "Hey, I love you, Ky. Everything is going to be alright."

"I believe you." We turned to face the justice of the peace we hired to officiate the wedding.

The rest was a blur of softly spoken words meant to let each other and everyone else know how committed we are to making this marriage work. When that was over, and Alex was told he could kiss the bride, Tabby said, "Me first." Her soft lips touched my cheek, then she whispered the sweetest words, "I love you, Mommy."

The tears couldn't be held back, and I let them flow as I kissed her cheek. "I love you, too, my baby girl."

Alex put Tabby down, and Carla took her hand as Alex took me into his arms. His eyes held mine as he inched closer. "I will always love you, Ky Arlen."

"I will always love you, too, Dr. Arlen." Our lips touched, and fire ripped through me.

I'm Alex's wife!

He picked me up and took me down the aisle as everyone cheered. It was magical! And when I saw Rebecca Vanderhaven dabbing away tears, I knew she approved mouthing, "Congratulations."

I mouthed back, "Thank you."

The fact Tabby's grandparents had come to our wedding made us glad. We could all become family now. That's all I ever wanted was for us to become: a family who loved and cared about each other.

Alex stopped as we got to the end of the green carpet and turned to face the crowd. "Thank you all for coming. We're blessed to have so many people care about us. Adding Ky to my family is one of the best things I've ever done. And we've got news, too." He nodded in Tabby's direction. "Tabby, you can give everyone the news now, honey."

Tabby held her arms up to Carla. "Pick me up, Carla?"

"Sure." Carla picked her up and kissed her on the cheek. "You're adorable."

"Thank you," Tabby said. "You're pretty, too."

Andrew, who was Alex's best man, nodded. "Yeah, she is."

Tabby giggled. "Uncle Andrew likes you."

I laughed, then called out, "The big news, Tabby. Come on, people are waiting, and your dad can't hold me like this for much longer."

"Can too," Alex said then lifted me even higher. "See? No problem at all."

"Be careful, Daddy!" Tabby shouted. "Okay, the big news." Everyone got quiet. All eyes were on Tabby as she said, "We're having a baby!"

More cheers rang out, and Alex kissed me once more. "We're going to be a great family, Ky. I promise."

And I believe him.

The End

Did you like this book? Then you'll LOVE Dirty Little Virgin: A Submissives' Secrets Novel 1

School is in session, and the lessons are rock hard!

She wants to write about the domme and my world.

And I'm supposed to teach her, not take her.
But her feisty manner begs to be tamed.
Her innocence begs to be taken.
I know my whip can bring her into submission.
Her young body begs for my harsh and experienced touch.
I'll train her to accept pain to gain pleasure.
The seclusion is temporary, as is our contract.
But what if I want something more permanent?

I'm not supposed to fall for my subs but I seem to be breaking all my own rules...

Start Reading Dirty Little Virgin

https://books2read.com/u/4jarKo

SNEAK PEEK - JADE

Start Reading Dirty Little Virgin

ROMANCE HAS BEEN in my blood since I was only a girl of sixteen. An avid reader of anything in the romance genre, I'm especially keen on the darker side of the romantic spectrum, the side where pain and pleasure meet in an ebbing and flowing stream of both calm and frantic nuances. A place where sin and evil meet with good and innocence, leaving their residue on each.

My curiosities have come all the way to the surface, and they won't allow me to shove them down any longer. I sit at my computer, searching the vast Internet to find someone who will help me. I need help to understand the reality that is BDSM, something that won't leave my mind.

The books I've read are great, enjoyable, and pleasing. But I think they're purely fictional, with little to do with the reality of that lifestyle. And I want to know more about it all; the why's, where's, and how's of the whole thing. Why do people do it? Where do they find others who want the same things they do? How do they take society's sideways glares that let them know everyone knows what they're doing, and that most think it's disgusting?

What immoral behavior is has been adjusted since the days of old when women wore nightgowns that covered them from their necks to their feet, and men were covered too. Small slits were made in the front for sexual activity, an activity that was not for pleasure but for procreation and procreation alone.

Masturbation, if one was caught doing such a horrible thing, was more than merely frowned upon. One was punished for it, and harshly, at that. Nowadays when one is punished, per their requests, mind you, they're deemed immoral. It's a common belief that if one practices BDSM or any variety of that, then the person must've had a bad upbringing or something terrible happened to them. Most people think something sexually abusive occurred.

I have to admit that I have favored that mindset. Recently, for reasons I cannot explain, I've had other thoughts about the people who practice the lifestyle. I just can't imagine why anyone would want to dole out punishment or receive it, as an adult. But deep in the recesses of my heart, I long to understand. The core belief resides in me that not all who seek out this type of attention have been broken in one way or another.

Being an erotic author is my dream, my passion. I simply love to go away in my head to worlds where anything is possible. Worlds where an ordinary woman can meet up with an abnormally handsome, viral, and of course, heavily muscled man. He would be filthy rich and just plain filthy in the bedroom, or any room, really.

The world of erotic romance is where I dwell so often in my mind. Damsels in distress are no longer acceptable heroines. No, today's heroines are smart, sharp as tacks in the wit department, strong in all ways, and take-no-shit kind of broads. The majority of these fictional women aren't looking for love; they seem to stumble upon it. And with that little stumble, they find themselves in the arms of a man.

Not any man will do in today's erotic romances. He must be alpha, clean to his core. In many of these novels, for some reason, our hero loves to hit women. And they love to be hit by him. And that is where my writer's brain has found a dilemma.

I can see falling for a big, strong, handsome man. Who can't?

But falling for one who wants to tie you up and beat your ass while you cook his dinner and iron his clothes, well, I can't see it at all. BDSM makes no sense to me, and I'm striving to make sense of it. For my career!

I was a writer before I was anything else. I told stories before I could read. I looked at scenes and made up why things were going as they were. Making up stories has always been like second nature to me.

Being only one year away from graduating with a Master's Degree in Creative Arts at Bangor University in North Wales, United Kingdom, I'm dangerously close to the part of life where I will need to make my own living in this world. Soon to be cut off from my father's dime, I have to focus, and that means I must have some belief in what I'm writing about, or I will never see my dreams come true.

My dreams aren't huge. I want to see my name on the cover of books. Oh! And best sellers' lists as well, of course. I don't want to be a mediocre writer. I want to be one of those authors who goes the distance to get to the meat of the story, somewhat like a reporter, only I want to get creative with my truths. I want to make my characters, and the world they live in, seem realistic while having fantasy-like lives.

And there is little to no reality in normal women finding men with voracious sexual appetites and a penchant for beating them. So, here I am, searching the Internet, hoping no one ever looks at my browser's history and thinks I'm a woman of ill repute. I am far from that.

At the ripe old age of twenty-three, I haven't found Mr. Right. And by that, I mean my cherry is still intact. I'm not a prude, though one might think that. I'm just very into my own head a lot of the time. A writer's thing, my professors tell me. I've been told I'm normal, for a writer.

Socially, I am a bit inept. Sure, I talk with ease to others, part of my reporter's instinct, I suppose. But I share little about myself, preferring to steer people in directions that allow me to learn more about them, rather than talking about myself.

With a click of my mouse, an awkward picture fills my computer screen. A woman deep throating an enormous penis!

Hurrying to get the picture off my screen, I notice the small writing at the bottom of the page. It's about some auction that's about to come up. Only after seeing that do I notice that the link I clicked on that took me to this sexual place belongs to BDSM club in Portland, Oregon, in the States.

Several clicks later, I find out this place is a haven for those types of people, and there are many clubs in that city. It's the number one city in America to find things of this nature. And it seems like the perfect place to begin my search for people who might be helpful enough to be truthful with me and offer me more insight into the dark world that's shrouded in mystery.

Another click sends me to a picture of a naughty young woman wearing leather clothing and holding her hand to her mouth as she looks surprised. I suppose she never saw the man coming who's behind her. Hard to believe, as he has a whip in his hand, and it's aimed for her round and firm ass. Somehow, he's surprised her with what he's about to do.

No fear is in her eyes. No tears from pain. Only a surprised look covers her pretty face. The man wears a firm expression on his ruggedly handsome facade. I can hear him now, in my mind, "Gertie, you have this coming to you. You forgot the salt in my soup again."

I giggle to myself, as that was an actual line in one of the novels I read, recently. Even then I thought it was silly and dimwitted. If a man told me I was about to get whipped with an actual whip because of something so small and easily fixed with the jiggle of a salt shaker, I'd most likely laugh and walk away. He would obviously be an idiot and not worth my attention or time.

My mind is too strong, and so is my will, to ever be involved in any of that stuff. But it's such a fantasy for many women that it bears investigating. My first novel in the erotic realm should have more than a grain of truth to it. I want some real grit mixing in with the fairy tale of a story I will create. None of that phony crap!

I wonder if I can find a real Dom or Master to ask questions to. I wonder if any of them would even want to take time away from whipping asses to talk to a lowly, vanilla virgin about things she knows little to nothing about.

Doubt clouds my vision as I sit back and gaze at the next thing that's popped up on my screen. A couple of women, clad in nothing but black panties, stand with their backs to a whip-wielding man who wears a black mask and looks like he's about to bring down the rain on them both.

"Run, you morons," I say out loud, as I notice an open door to their right.

Is it humanly possible to stand still and take the pain of a whip when you're steps away from escape?

Is it possible that, in some people, the need to feel pain is overwhelming, like a drug addict who hates the after effects of a certain drug but can't stop taking it?

The sharp eyes of the women as they look over their shoulders while holding hands, waiting for the whip to meet one of their bodies, haunt me. How can they be so bright eyed with pain on the way?

If I see a hot burner on the stove, I don't touch it. If I saw a man running wildly down the street with his belt in his hand, striking out at people, I'd hide. So why do some seek this out?

And what chance do I have of finding even one of the people who practice BDSM who would be willing to help me understand them? And why would they want to?

I'm offering no compensation for their time. I'm offering nothing. I merely want to satisfy my own curiosity, nothing more than that. I want to use what I'm given to make money, as a matter of fact.

No, it's doubtful that I will be able to find anyone in the BDSM scene to answer my questions. Perhaps I should end this silliness.

Maybe I should put this idea to rest and focus on romantic comedy, instead. That would be so much easier, wouldn't it?

Pierce

Her ass sways as she leaves the room. Strands of leather cover it, and red marks cover the places the straps don't. After an hour of cuddling my sub for the evening, Tasha, she feels safe enough to leave my company in the private room I rented at The Dungeon of Decorum. She wanted no sex, only punishment. And I gave her what she asked for, like any good Dom would.

Relaxing on the small bed in the room made for torturing the flesh of submissives, I can't help but recall the first time I came here. It was a mere three years ago, yet it feels like a century.

Bogged down in business, I was burning out fast. Being the new CEO of Waterson Mutual, a business finance company in Portland, Oregon, I was trying to prove my worth to the board, busting my ass far more than I needed to. And it was catching up to me.

Grant Jamison became my friend and eventual hero. Older than me by five years, he took me under his wing and taught me that work is great, but one should always leave time for play.

Grant's idea of play was very different from what my idea was. I thought he was suggesting playing racquetball with him and the friends he talked about. What he brought me into was far more serious than a ballgame.

In the matter of one month, I was inducted into the brotherhood of the Dominants at a local BDSM club, aptly named The Dungeon of Decorum, a place I now visit often.

Being a Dom comes naturally to me, as if I was born to lead, teach, and rule women. At thirty-five, I've been told I should be settling down and finding a woman to marry. I've been told I can keep my dark hobby a secret and lead a normal life in every other way, but that sounds boring to me.

Being a part of the club I belong to means I can't divulge any information about myself or any other members. We're an eclectic group of men, who happen to all be wealthy. With that in common, we all have to hide our secret lives. After all, who would want a mayor, a banker, or a statesman who's into such dark things?

I was astonished by the faces I saw upon visiting the club for the first time. Men from all over the U.S. come to the club. Auctions are especially busy, as not only men come from everywhere, but so do the women who are auctioned off.

Personally, I've never bought a woman. I've never had an ongoing thing with any of the subs. I prefer one-time scenes. I follow up with the women I've played with for about a week's time, then it's on to other things. Things like other women with other needs, fetishes, and desires.

Studying techniques extensively has earned me the reputation for being one of the best Doms if one is looking for an excellent experience in bondage. My kinks are bondage, suspension, cupping, impact play, and power exchange, all of which I am particularly good at.

More than once, I've been called driven— in business, in bed, and in my personal kinks. If it interests me, I dive into it head first and don't come up until I'm saturated in knowledge.

I've had three serious relationships in my life. Two of them ended because of my incessant drive. Janet, in college, said I was too into my studies and not enough into her. So, she dumped me.

Leah, my second girl, lived with me when I first started working in the finance world. I had to devote most of my time to work. I wanted to move up quickly. After a year, she called it quits too, another woman who told me I didn't spend enough time with her.

Tracy was a gold digger who lured me into what she thought might be a trap. It was the first year I broke the billion-dollar mark on my yearly income. The daughter of a grocery store janitor, Tracy wanted more out of life. I asked her to move into my spanking new mansion with me. I showered her with gifts and tried my best to make time for her.

Tracy was one beautiful woman. Long blonde hair with golden streaks hung to her tiny waist. Bright blue eyes spoke to my heart, telling me I'd found an angel. But she turned out to be a demon instead.

Not wanting to get into having a family at that time, I was an avid condom user. When she came to me with a pregnancy test stick that had a couple of lines in it, she told me she was pregnant. With my child!

I'm no idiot; I know condoms aren't one hundred percent effective, but she had also told me she was taking a birth control shot. Anyone can imagine how I felt: shocked, as well as disbelieving.

Tracy was furious when I took her to a doctor and stayed with her as she took the pregnancy test at the physician's office. It came back negative, and I knew then and there that the woman was trying to force me into marriage. I had no choice; I dumped her.

And after her, I've had no desire to deal with women for an extended period of time again. I'm not broken. I'm just too busy to want to deal with all that comes with a relationship.

At the club, I can find women who want whatever I do at the time, anything from letting out aggression to cuddling and fulfilling that need. And not one of the women I've been with since joining the club has asked anything more from me than I am willing to give. A relief is what it is.

No games are played. In our world, we communicate far more than in the normal world, the world with innuendos, cat and mouse shenanigans, and downright lies to get into relationships that are racked with turmoil.

Women have been taught things by society that go against nature. I never realized that until I found the BDSM world. Things like fighting hard to be above men, a thing that's insane, have been shoved into their minds.

Women and men are different. We were put here to serve different purposes. There isn't one of us who is better than the other. And one cannot exist without the other. Society has interfered with the natural order of things. And I, for one, am tired of dealing with women who fight nature.

A sense of calmness took me over soon after beginning this lifestyle. There's no arguing, no manipulations, no flirting to get into a woman's panties now. That shit is history. In the club, I can go up to any woman I'd like to, as long as she doesn't belong to a man who prefers her to be with only him, and I can be frank with her. I can tell her what I'd like to do with and to her, and she's free to accept it or not.

If she's into it, then we discuss every last detail about what we want to exchange with one another and plan out our scene. The planning is like foreplay. One gets hot and horny while discussing the details. Keeping our hands to ourselves can be hard as we describe what we want. But I prefer to hold back any physical connection until we get into our scene. It builds anticipation and makes for a better session.

A rap on the darkly stained oak door to the private room takes me out of my thoughts. "Come in."

Grant pushes the door open. He's got his arm around a tall, lithe brunette with tons of makeup on. "Hey, Pierce, this one here wants someone to watch us. You game?"

I slide off the bed and pull on my black lounge pants. "Sure. Am I a loud member of the audience or a quiet creeper?"

"Loud," she tells me as I make my way to them. She strokes my cheek as she peers into my eyes. "My, you are a looker. And that body. Mmmm."

Taking her hand away from my face, as I don't allow touch until we're in the act, I let her know, "If you like what you see, we can talk sometime soon about what you need, baby."

"I need you," she whispers, making my groin thump.

"We'll see how well you take what my friend dishes out before you and I talk about what it is you need." I step to one side and allow Grant to lead the party to wherever he has planned.

Grant winks at me. "Perhaps you could show me your flogging

technique on her if she's all right with that. I've heard you've developed it so it's better than most Doms'."

The way the woman, wearing only a thin, white, silk robe, looks over her shoulder at me, tells me she'd like that.

"Sure, I can show you."

"I cannot wait," she purrs.

A growl fills my throat as I think about how she's about to feel. "Baby, we're about to take you to the Amber Zone."

Jade

The night is long. I toss and turn most of it. Dreams of whips and chains fill the hours, along with men in dark shadows who call out for me to stop running.

Getting out of bed, I rub the sleep from my eyes and make my way to the shower. My flat is small, and I'm tired of looking at the same walls each day. Summer is nearly here, and I want to go on holiday somewhere, get out of my country for a couple of months and see some other place.

The water's hot, making steam fill the tiny water closet. Steeping into the standup shower, my body jerks as the heated water hits it. "Ow!" I turn down the heat and make the water's temperature more compatible with my skin.

Memories of the dreams which plagued me bounce around in my head. In them I was different. I was unafraid, yet not allowing myself to be drawn in by the husky, deep voices of the men.

The plum shampoo smells great and helps to wake me up. After a shot of something with caffeine in it, I should be good to go. It's the weekend, and I have nothing to do but study for my finals. One more week of school, then I'll be free.

I'm not one of those creatures who freaks out over finals. I know my stuff, as I pay attention in class and have an honest interest in the subject matter. That always helps.

Turning off the water, I step out and towel off. Throwing on a fluffy pink robe, I wrap the towel around my hair in a turban-like fashion and make my way back into my bedroom. A set of sweats will do for my day of studying and chilling out.

After getting dressed, I stroll out to the kitchen to make some coffee and pop a bagel into the toaster. Taking the cream cheese out of the fridge, I notice my laptop sitting on the kitchen counter where I left it last night.

Before I went to bed, I told myself that I'd forget about trying to find anyone to answer my BDSM questions. The realization that no one would waste his time with me settled into my head.

The dreams have sparked my insatiable curiosity once again and I find myself drawn to the silver laptop. I open it and turn it on. It buzzes and whirrs as it comes to life.

My attention is taken away from the device as the toaster pops up my bagel and I set about pouring a cup of coffee and getting my little breakfast ready to eat. Sitting at the table, I take my first bite and look at my laptop again.

"Oh, what the hell." I get up and grab it, placing it on the tabletop and typing in the search engine I like to use when doing research.

Tapping in a simple 'BDSM society,' I sit back and let the engine find something for me to read while I eat half of my bagel and sip the stout black coffee. A directory of sites comes up on the screen, and I tap the first one. A list appears at the top of the page. The title explains they're things used to play with. The first item is a spreader bar. The picture looks innocuous enough. But the description says the bar can be made of metal or wood, and it's used to keep the submissive spread open. It can be utilized on either the wrists or the ankles, and it can even be hung from the ceiling.

"Oh, my!"

Why on Earth would anyone willingly be held in that position?

Oh, well. On to the next thing: medical restraints. A set of four small leather belts is used to hold a person to the bed. I have to ask myself: if it's all so great, why does one have to be bound to the bed?

Next, I see something called a monoglove. The poor girl has her arms behind her back and is wrapped with a leather glove-like thing. She's helpless to move her arms. Again, I must ask myself, why?

Not only does it look constricting and uncomfortable, it seems silly to me. Does the Dom need to keep his sub's hands away from him or something?

Moving on, I find a muzzle gag, a penis gag, and a ring gag; they all look more than a bit uncomfortable. I'm left wondering if I would actually choke if the penis gag was put into my mouth and strapped there. I definitely think I would!

A medieval-looking device is next. It's used to hold a person's nose, pulling it backward so their head is pulled back and their mouth opens. It's called a nose hook, and I really have no idea why it would be considered a sexual device. It looks like a thing one would use to get a child to accept medicine when they fight about taking it.

"Oh! I get it now!" A blush heats my cheeks as I think about being forced to open my mouth and having a man's cock placed into it.

If I were a man, though, I still wouldn't trust the object to stop my submissive from clamping down on my dick. And if she has to be forced to accept it, then why's she there in the first place?

I just keep finding more questions to ask!

Plastic wrap is next on the list, and I see that it's used to wrap up the sub like a mummy. How inexpensive that is, and how odd that anyone thought of that. I can hear the odd couple now: "Honey, can you get the plastic wrap from the kitchen? I think I'll wrap it around you tonight so I can have my way with you."

And the daft woman would run off to fetch the item without a thought in her empty head. No, I just don't get it at all!

Something called a posture collar is next on this insane list. It's just like the white collars one wears when they have a neck injury. Perhaps it's used to aid in the protection of the neck when being beaten like an animal. The woman who has it on looks equally as uncomfortable as any person I've seen wearing one because they had to.

So, I am left with more questions than I previously had, and my curiosity is banging on my brain to get the answers it requires. But I close the laptop and try to focus on what I really need to be doing, studying for my finals.

The chair I'm sitting in is made of wood and not comfortable in the least, with its rigid back. Studying goes out the window as I close my eyes and imagine being strapped to the chair with leather medical restraints. A wide posture collar wrapped around my neck makes me sit up straight. A spreader bar holds my legs open and a monoglove pins my arms behind my back. Even the fantasy is constricting and awkward. I open my eyes and laugh as I think about letting anyone do such things to me.

And those things aren't anywhere nearly as horrible as the whips and chains. My mind is right back where it's been for the past several months: bondage, brutality, and why anyone would allow that to happen to them. What type of beasts want to do that to someone?

In the romance novels, women easily fall in love with their tormentors. Why?

If a man did even half of the things to me that I've read about, I think I'd kill him in his sleep and not have an ounce of guilt over it. To fall in love with such a beastly person is a thing I cannot imagine.

With the first sting of the whip, I'd vow to kill the motherfucker. I'm sure I would. A Dom would have to use a muzzle or gag on me, as I'd threaten his very existence as he tortured me. And when he set me free, which he'd have to do eventually, well, he'd be the one running scared. Of that, I am certain.

Perhaps I'd be better suited as the dominator. But then again, I could never bring myself to hit a person. Hurting someone's feelings is a thing I hate. Actually hurting someone physically isn't a thing I could do or condone.

So how am I supposed to talk to a person who actively does these things without judging them?

If I ask a question such as, "How does it make you feel to hit a woman?" and get a truthful answer, then what will I do?

If a man were to tell me that he gets joy out of hitting a woman, then I'd detest him. A man who bound a woman, then hit her and took her sexually, well, he'd be a person I couldn't stand.

So what the hell am I doing? Why am I thinking about trying to talk to someone who I think is evil? What the hell is wrong with me? And what would my family think of me for even contemplating this?

Sitting back, I try to rationalize my thoughts. Like a reporter, I don't have to agree with anything when I'm trying to get information. I can ask questions, get my answers, and move on from the monster.

It's not as if I'm going to ask some Dom to take me on and show me what happens in their dark world. I'd never do that!

My hand moves to the laptop and pulls it open. It's like my will has taken over as I type 'BDSM Clubs' into the search engine. My fingers hesitate as I see the first link to a club with an actual website. It's called "The Dungeon of Decorum", and I click it.

Looking over the page that opens, I find a message board and type in Is there anyone in this club who'd like to help me learn more about the real world of BDSM?

Now to see if anyone wants to respond ...

Pierce

Birds chirp, waking me from a deep sleep. Blinking my eyes to shield them from the bright sunlight that's pouring through my pale green, sheer- curtained window, I stretch and yawn with the onset of the weekend. With no plans made, I think I'll make myself a healthy breakfast of oatmeal and wheat toast, then head to the gym. Maybe I'll just let the day take me wherever it wants to.

Moving to the bathroom, I turn on the shower, letting the steamy water heat the cold tiles. Multiple jets shoot the water out, hitting almost the entire surface of the tiled walls. Padding over to the sink, I brush my teeth, floss, then rinse with mouthwash.

Into the shower I go, pouring an expensive shampoo I found online last week into my palm. It smells like leather and sandalwood, making me feel exceptionally masculine. In no time at all, I'm bright-eyed and bushy-tailed and dry off, then dress in casual clothing. Jeans, a T-shirt, and running shoes will suffice.

Heading downstairs to the kitchen, I find the fridge well-stocked. Edith, my house manager, has made sure I'm ready to cook for myself through the weekend, like I always do. I give the staff every weekend off. I prefer to be alone in my home when I'm off. They come in after I leave for work each weekday and are gone before I come home.

During the week, I take my meals in town. Most of the time, I get home around eight and usually hit the hay pretty early. I'm a faithful subscriber to the idea that early to bed and early to rise makes a man healthy, wealthy, and wise. So far, it's worked wonders for me!

After making my breakfast, I take it to the table and open up my laptop to see what's going on around Portland this weekend. As always, I check the club's website first to see if any of the subs have posted anything I might be interested in.

The name Jade Thomas is the first thing I see as I scan the message board. I've never seen that name on here before. And she's asked a question.

Is there anyone in this club who'd like to help me learn more about the real world of BDSM?'

"Jade Thomas," I say out loud. "And what does this young lady want to know, I wonder?"

Without hesitation, I ask my own question, What do you want to know more about our world for?

I begin to eat my oatmeal as I wait to see if she'll answer me. It takes no time before I see her response. Just curious. And is your real name Dr. Power?

Laughing, I type back, No, we don't use our real names on this site. But I bet you did, Jade Thomas.

Eating my toast, I watch the screen, eager to see her reply.

That is my real name. What's your real name? You see, I'm looking for a person who will be honest with me about the goings on in the BDSM scene. If you can't be honest enough to tell me your name, then I shouldn't waste any more of your time.

Thinking about the fact that she might be wasting my time, I ask, Where are you from, Jade?

She's quick to answer, The United Kingdom. If you're worried about me outing you to society or something like that, you needn't worry.

"A Brit," I say to myself. She's far enough away, I doubt her knowing my real name would hurt a thing. I type in, Pierce Langford.

Thank you, Pierce Langford. First, I'd like to tell you that I'm majoring in creative writing at a university in North Wales. My goal is to become a romance author. I'd like to specialize in the erotic genre. But I need some information about certain topics. Topics like the BDSM scene. I don't fully understand it. Oh, who am I kidding, I don't understand it all. Are you by chance a Dom?

I am. Why, you looking for one? I type in.

Purely to ask questions to, nothing more than that. Are you up to answering some questions for me, sir?

Her use of the term sir lets me know she's a respectful woman. But I should find out how old she is before I give her such information. Before I divulge information that might warp a young mind, I need to know your age and your sexual experience, Jade.

Thoughtful of you, sir. My age is 23, and my sexual experience is limited to masturbation. I am a virgin.

"Holy fuck!"

My mouth's watering with the thought that she's a virgin. I wonder what she looks like!

Cool. Not a problem. As long as you're of age and have an inkling about what kinds of answers you'll be getting from me, I'm good with answering your questions. So, shoot me one.

An entire minute goes by before anything appears. Is there a private area we can do this, sir?

I think about it for a moment, then decide to give her my personal touch. Do you have a Skype account?

I do. I prefer not to video conference though, if you don't mine.'

"Hmm, must be an ugly duckling. That's most likely why she's still a virgin."

I type in, Not to worry, I won't try to video chat with you. My number is 999-987-0099. I'll be waiting for your message, Jade.

In no time at all, she's messaged me, and a little ding comes from my phone. I pull it up on my computer to make typing easier and find even her profile picture on the site is nothing but a red rose. I find it funny, as my picture is a black rose with thorns on it.

Hi, Pierce. Do you mind if I call you that? I don't want to establish a submissive relationship with you and just realized that by calling you sir, I am doing just that.

I chuckle as I write back, You may call me that. So, what's your first question?

Much too quickly she sends back, Do you like to hit women?

Not happy with the question, I fire back, If this is some hater who wishes to berate me for what I am and enjoy doing, then you can go to hell!

Another quick response comes from her, No! Sorry. Please don't take any of my questions in an offensive manner. None of them are meant to offend you. All are meant merely to learn about this lifestyle. Nothing more than that. I simply want to know if you took up this practice because you had a fetish about hitting people or women in general.

Letting my anger subside, I give it a minute to settle. She's just curious. I have to remember she's young and naïve.

This is not a thing I started because of a need to hit anyone. I was having difficulty at work. I needed an outlet. I was introduced to this world. I joined this club and found that submissives wanted certain things done to them. I took classes and learned how to give them what they asked for. And I became good at it. You see, some people like pain, Jade. Some people crave it. I administer the thing they feel they need. I do it with them in mind. Not for myself.

Three minutes tick by before she sends me another question. Do you have an exclusive relationship with your sub?

I don't. I never have.

Do you have a commitment phobia? Or anything in your past that caused you to enjoy this lifestyle?

Weighing the question so I can answer truthfully, I finally type, Perhaps I do have a commitment issue. I wouldn't call it a phobia. And nothing is in my past that's messed up my mind, contrary to what a lot of people think about us.

How old are you? she asks.

35.

Again, some time goes by before she writes anything else. Then the words appear on the screen. I'd like to be clear on what type of Dom I'm talking to. Are you a heterosexual, Pierce?

I am. Are you?

Yes. I only ask as I want to write M/F romances and spending time talking to a man who likes men would do me no good. Do Doms only dole out punishments? And if not, have you received any?

One can play both ends of the spectrum if they want to. There are no rules stating that once a sub always a sub or once a Dom always a Dom. When I was in training, I was hit by my trainer. That way I would know what it felt like to be hit with the items I was taught to use. But no sub has ever hit me. Nor do I plan on that ever happening. I rule.

The pause she takes is so long, I begin to wonder if she's decided to stop our interview. Then I see her next question.

Are you the type who wants to rule everything? And if so, why do you not have an exclusive sub?

Her question has me pondering it. Do I want to rule everything? I have no idea. I've never done that. The two live-in girlfriends I had certainly needed a firmer hand than I had back then. If I found a woman that I wanted to keep around, I think I'd like to make the rules.

With my answer, I type, Your question is a first for me. I looked deep inside myself and found I would like to rule if I ever found a sub I wanted to keep with me for any length of time. I prefer things certain ways and would train a sub to do things the way I like them done.

Do you feel women are inferior?

Her question nearly knocks the wind out of my sails.

Quickly, I reply, Not at all. You see, most of us in the BDSM world don't think on those terms. Women and men have their roles to play in life. With the rise of women's liberation, women have lost more than they've gained. Once upon a time, women were the esteemed nurturers of the family, the keepers of the children, the homes, and their husbands. They made sure all things on the home front were taken care of well and were proud of their job. Men went to work and provided money and security, not only in the financial form but also in the protection department. They made and upheld the rules and used different forms of discipline to enforce them.

I give pause to allow my words to sink into her head. With the way things have changed in the last fifty or so years, most women balk at this way of thinking, calling it ancient and useless. I wait to see how Jade will respond.

I've never thought about it like that.

A smile moves over my lips. "Good girl."

Jade

Only a few questions in, and already he has me thinking differently. What he says is true. Women had it much easier before we decided we wanted to be equals in all ways. Not so long ago, women stayed home with the kids. They didn't have to worry about work or paying bills. That was the man's job.

Nowadays, mothers and wives go off to work and some have to actually leave their homes for days at a time. That's left a generation of children who've been raised by strangers. People who work at the many daycare facilities that have sprung up all over the industrialized world now are responsible for the caring and nurturing of most babies and children that mothers once took care of all on their own.

Women now depend on their husbands to step up and take care of the children too. All chores are shared, and while that seems fair, I've seen a good number of frazzled parents in my time. Both are sleep deprived. Both have the weight of making sure the bills are paid on their backs. And both have the responsibility of finding great jobs and keeping them, no matter how much pressure comes with that.

Men's minds have also been changed. Most men, back in the day, wouldn't have their wives working. They'd have been considered deadbeats or losers if they sent their wives to work outside the home. Nowadays, it's expected. And in a few words, Pierce has brought this home to me. How odd that I never thought of it before.

I can see Pierce's side. Then again, as a woman with a brain that begs for knowledge and gentle pressure to expand and learn more all the time, I can see why women fought to be let out of the house. I have also seen stay-at-home mothers who resemble zombies and have difficulty putting a sentence together, much less being able to have conversations with other adults.

There are pros and cons either way you decide to live. That's just a simple fact of life.

My next question is a bit hairy, and I hope I don't offend the man again as I type, I now understand how you think about the sexes. What I don't understand is where the domination comes into play. Nor the physical punishments that come along with BDSM. Can you explain this to me?

The physical punishments are accepted or rejected by each submissive. It is she who helps shape the agreements that are made between a Dom and his sub. Another thing you must not be aware of is that submissives hold all the cards. One simple word is all it takes to stop anything. It's not quite the torturous world people make it out to be. And nothing happens to a sub that they're against. That would be illegal, wouldn't it?

I suppose it would. So these agreements are the contracts that bind the sub to the Dom? I ask.

They are, he answers me quickly. But you must keep in mind that even a signed contract that's been painstakingly worked out between the two parties still doesn't give the Dom the right to proceed with any punishment or action if the sub doesn't want it. No matter if she agreed to it in the first place or not. And a good Dom doesn't want to inflict any pain, or pleasure, for that matter, that his submissive doesn't want.

I find it hard to believe the man. I mean, he could tell me whatever he wants to. Because what woman wants to be ruled over and beaten? So, I ask, Pierce, what types of women want to be treated this way?

There are women from various walks of life who seek this lifestyle, maybe not all the time, but some of the time. You see, when you get into this world, you find that anything is okay. If you want to live this way all the time, then you can. If you want to dabble, you can do that too. There are no set rules, except those that govern our society. SSC—safe, sane, consensual—was put into use to make sure all who are involved in this type of lifestyle have a level of protection. Clubs keep the members in line too. That's why it's always a good idea to join one and only get involved with people who are part of one. There are enforcers who make sure no one is hurt beyond the point they've asked to be. If you're interested in being an onlooker, you can join a local club in your area and let them know what you want. We have voyeurs too. But I must warn you, it's not easy to watch if you have no idea about what the people truly feel. It looks brutal, after all.

That it does, Pierce. And about that. You said you were hit when you were training to be a Dom. Can you explain why anyone would want that?

While I never got to the state of euphoria, I've heard it described as flying. It's a high that one gets when endorphins swarm the brain. At that point, when you add in sexual stimulation, it's mind blowing. Some have described it as an out-of-body experience that took them to new levels in their minds and souls. You can see how one would enjoy that and seek it over and over again.

Yet you've never done that? I ask, as I have no idea why he'd want to only inflict pain and get nothing out of it.

I'm more of a giver than a taker. Always have been.

You make it sound noble, what you do, I type.

In a way, it is. Can you imagine if you had this itch in the middle of your back and you tried everything to scratch it yourself—rubbing your back on the door frame, trying to find a stick long enough to get to the exact spot you needed it to, but you couldn't reach it, no matter what you did? Then along came some person who could easily scratch that itch for you, but he didn't want to inflict any type of pain on you. If you think about it, running one's sharp fingernails across another person's flesh sounds painful. Yet it eases the itch, relieving the person of their problem.

"Wow!" I say to myself. "This guy's kind of deep. I didn't expect this."

He goes on, adding, A doctor also causes his patient pain on many occasions in order to treat an ailment. Does anyone consider him immoral?

My mind is swarming with more questions, yet I feel as if he's winning me over to his way of thinking. So, I ask, When you're hitting your subs, do you get sexually stimulated? I ask this because a doctor doesn't get turned on by giving his patient pain. Nor does anyone get turned on by helping someone scratch an itch they can't reach.

Time goes by, and I think he might be trying to figure out how to word his answer. Finally, the screen lights up.

Jade, you ask exemplary questions. The fact is that I do get turned on by what I do. Feminine screams and moans make my cock hard. But if you'd like to know the truth, your questions have stirred an erection too. You see, the libido is an odd thing. When you're young, the slightest breeze across your dick can make it go hard. As we get older, other things cause sexual excitement. A soft whisper uttered into an ear, a touch from a beautiful woman, a stimulating conversation between strangers. I bet you're a remarkable young woman.

He seems to be flirting, which has me nervous for some reason. It's stupid. The man is thousands of miles away from me. He can't do a thing to me and here I am, fidgeting in my seat, my nipples beginning to pebble, and heat filling my crotch.

I type, How are you able to seduce me so quickly?

Are you wet for me, Jade?

My heart pounds as I type back, I seem to be.

Run your hand into your panties, Jade.

His simple command has my hand moving without me thinking about it. I feel the heat radiating from my vagina. Then I use my right hand to type, Perhaps you could take your enlarged cock into your hand, Pierce.

It's already there, he lets me know. Run a finger into that virgin hole of yours. Pump it a few times and say my name as you do that.

My cheeks heat as my pussy goes wet and I do as he's told me to. This is not me! This isn't a thing I've ever done!

But no one can see me, and no one will ever know I did such a thing. So I pump my finger and say his name out loud, "Pierce, Pierce, Pierce!"

His name rolls off my tongue as my eyes close and I keep going until the sound of another message comes in. I open my eyes to find he's written, Now use your other hand and pinch the shit out of your nipple and hold it there even though it hurts.

I look at his words and wonder why I'd do such a thing. The fingering feels nice; the pinching won't. But for some odd reason, I push my shirt up and pull my bra up too, then pinch my nipple with my right hand while I finger myself with the other and let out a shriek. Not of pain, but of something else. Pure bliss. Pure and unadulterated pleasure.

My God. How has he corrupted me already?

Start Reading Dirty Little Virgin

If you want to read the entire Season of Desire Series at a discount, you can get the complete box set by clicking here.

https://books2read.com/u/mZjAlR

www.ingramcontent.com/pod-product-compliance
Lightning Source LLC
LaVergne TN
LVHW021713060526
838200LV00050B/2636